ANNA SAYBURN LANE

Blackmail In Bloomsbury

A 1920s murder mystery

STARLING
STREET BOOKS

First published by Starling Street Books 2023

Copyright © 2023 by Anna Sayburn Lane

This novel is entirely a work of fiction. The names, characters and incidents portrayed in it are the work of the author's imagination. Any resemblance to actual living persons or events is entirely coincidental.

First edition

ISBN: 978-1-7395144-0-2

This book was professionally typeset on Reedsy.
Find out more at reedsy.com

To Kathy, in honour of Ritz Day

Foreword

This is the first of a new series of 1920s murder mystery adventures featuring assistant private investigator Marjorie Swallow. I hope you enjoy it.

A word about spelling: I'm a British author and the series is set in 1920s London, so I use UK English. Marjorie's employer Mrs Jameson is American, but she's lived in Europe for many years and doesn't object to Marjorie writing up her adventures in UK English.

You can find out more about my books, get free stories and a prequel novella, when you sign up to my Readers Club newsletter at annasayburnlane.com.

Chapter 1

Mrs Jameson swept into the suite, followed by three uniformed hotel porters carrying parcels. I brought up the rear, my feet aching. Yet again, we had failed to accomplish the major project of the day.

'Thank you, boys. You can put them over there.' Mrs Jameson waved towards the desk.

I gave the porters each a generous tip from her purse.

'Will there be anything else, Miss?' asked one.

'Could you send up some tea?' I asked. Mrs Jameson had collapsed into a well-upholstered armchair. I wasn't sure she'd last until dinnertime. 'And scones.'

'Yes, Miss Swallow.'

They departed and left us in the peace of the luxurious rooms. I hung our coats on the hall stand and sat at the walnut rolltop desk under the window that looked over Green Park. The billowing trees shimmered golden and bronze in the late afternoon sun. I unwrapped the books which Mrs Jameson had ordered from Hatchard's bookshop. They were a queer mixture: *A Complete Illustrated Modern Herbal*, the *Guide to Fingerprint Identification and Classification*, last year's *Criminal Law Casebook 1920 to 1921*. Mrs Jameson's library already contained books on poisons, anatomy texts, and a wide selection of 'penny dreadfuls' reporting on true crimes, from the brides in the bath horrors of 1915 to the many theories about the identity of Jack the Ripper. They were exactly the sort of books we were forbidden from reading at school, and I could only imagine the glee with which we would have seized on such a collection at Sydenham High. Working for a private lady detective was quite the education.

'Leave those alone, Marjorie, and sit down with me,' said Mrs Jameson.

I did as she instructed.

'I admit it, I'm disappointed,' she said.

My heart lurched. What had I done wrong? I had only begun working for Mrs Jameson two weeks previously. I'd been doing my best to anticipate her needs, dealing with the many cards and letters that arrived for her every day, accompanying her all over Mayfair as she viewed – and rejected – houses. But this was my first post as a personal secretary, and it was entirely possible I had unwittingly committed some terrible sin.

'I thought the Berkeley Square house would do it. Mr Tomkins was so enthusiastic,' she said.

I breathed. She was disappointed with the house, not with me.

'That is a pity, Mrs Jameson.' I'd been told not to call her Madam, that being a form of address she said was only used by shop girls. Having grown up as a draper's daughter and served in the shop from an early age, I had to bite my tongue a dozen times a day.

It was hard to see what was wrong with the houses we had viewed. They all looked like palaces to me, with imposing white pillars outside, black and white chequered hallways like

2

so many enormous chess boards, sweeping staircases and wide bow windows.

'What's wrong with these places?' she asked. The question was rhetorical. 'There's no life in any of them. Cold, cold, cold. Like those big iced wedding cakes you see in the windows of bakeries, which never change because they're hard icing over empty wooden boxes. Nothing inside, no substance.'

She frowned. 'I'd thought it would be easy to find somewhere. Everyone tells me that all the grand families are giving up their London houses. But I suppose that's why these gloomy squares seem so lifeless.'

That was true. Half the houses in the squares we'd visited today were shuttered. Perhaps they would re-open after Christmas, but many had a decidedly abandoned look.

'It's always like this in the autumn, though,' I said, trying to sound worldly-wise. As if my family shut up the flat over the shop in south London and moved to our country estate as soon as the shooting season started. I'd barely set foot in Mayfair before I began working for Mrs Jameson. It seemed like a very dull, Sunday-best part of town, with none of the attraction of the glamorous new department stores along Oxford Street, or the brightly lit theatres and restaurants of the West End.

'Perhaps.' I hoped Mrs Jameson wasn't going cold on her plan to find a permanent residence in London. I could quite understand why she might prefer the sunshine of Rome, or the elegance of Paris. She had ruled out her native America, 'Until they treat their citizens like adults and allow us to order a bourbon when we feel like it,' but she had lived in France and Italy for many years before deciding to move to England.

'Ah! Here is Graham to cheer us with tea and sympathy,' she said, as a discreet knock announced our favourite waiter.

I jumped up to open the door for Graham Hargreaves, who wheeled a laden trolley to the low table before the easy chairs.

'And how did you get on today, ladies?' he asked, pouring tea and setting out pots of jam and cream. His East End accent, unexpected in the rarefied surroundings of The Ritz, always made me smile.

'Hopeless, I'm afraid. You will have to put up with me a little longer.'

'Always a pleasure, Mrs Jameson.' He set a particularly juicy-looking scone in front of me, his kind face creasing into a conspiratorial smile. 'I'm worried you'll wear yourselves out with all this house-hunting. Why not stay here and let me look after you?'

I could think of nothing nicer than living in a luxury hotel under the care of Mr Hargreaves. He had been enormously kind to me right from the day of my interview. Indeed, the entire staff seemed determined to ensure Mrs Jameson's comfort.

Mrs Jameson laughed. 'What a tempting prospect! But I must have my own establishment. Just as soon as I can find somewhere that suits me.'

Graham reached below the crisp white linen on the trolley and laid five envelopes on the table, all addressed to Mrs Iris Jameson, c/o The Ritz Hotel, Piccadilly, London.

'These arrived by second post,' he said. 'Can I help you with anything else?'

Mrs Jameson was tackling her scones and her letters with equal enthusiasm.

'That'll be all for now.' She cast the first two letters aside with impatience and slit open the third. 'Oh! Well, I call that splendid.' She waved a stiff white card at me. 'At last – a dinner that is sure to be full of truly interesting people. Eileen always has a wonderfully mixed crowd. I'm so relieved. I thought I would die of boredom before the week was out.'

'That's nice,' I said, feeling rather crushed. Was my company really that dull? We had apprehended a murderer on our first day together, after all. I couldn't imagine what sort of excitement would top that.

Her sharp grey eyes slid sideways to me. 'I was excluding present company, but I shan't if you take umbrage, Miss Swallow.' She missed nothing. 'And you're coming with me, anyway. Thursday evening, two days' time. Miss Eileen Power is a fascinating woman. Her research on medieval convents opened a window on aspects of history rarely explored before. She's just back from China, I believe, and has taken a lecturing post at the London School of Economics. We met in Paris, at the Sorbonne, before the War.'

'Oh goodness. Are you sure?' Dinner with a bluestocking historian sounded terrifying. What on earth would I talk about? But I wouldn't be expected to talk, I reasoned. I could sit in dumb admiration, nodding politely, while the fascinating Eileen Power lectured us on medieval nuns.

'Certainly. The invitation is for two, and I would like you to meet some of my friends.'

Perhaps I would need to take down the lecture in shorthand. I'd had little enough call to use my vaunted secretarial qualifications in the past weeks. I decided to write to my old school friend Evelyn, who was studying law at Girton College in Cambridge. No doubt she could give me some advice on dealing with bluestockings.

Mrs Jameson frowned at the invitation. 'Where on earth is Mecklenburgh Square?'

Chapter 2

Two days later, we stepped out of the taxi at the house of the eminent historian in the bohemian Bloomsbury district of London. Mecklenburgh Square was rather elegant, terraces on three sides surrounding a garden with high-reaching plane trees. The house was tall, narrow, and dignified. Despite its proximity to the busy Gray's Inn Road, the square felt quiet, almost rural.

I was expecting our host to be a fusty old woman in tweed, maybe with whiskers on her chin and thick spectacles to peer through. The letter I received from Evelyn that morning had been little help.

'She's the most extraordinary woman!' she'd enthused. 'Quite brilliant. Lucky you! We were so sorry to lose her from Girton, but of course it's the university's fault for refusing women full degrees. Sickening! Anyway, you'll see.'

Her letter had made me even more nervous than I was already. It was all right for Evelyn; she was brainy. Her father was a lawyer and had always encouraged her to talk in a clever way. My father asks if I've swallowed a dictionary if I say more than 'Pass the salt,' at dinner. Anyway, my talents are more of a practical nature.

When I showed her what I planned to wear, Mrs Jameson

had sent me out to buy a new ready-made frock from Marshall and Snelgrove. I'd thought my navy plaid afternoon dress was quite respectable and suited for an academic gathering. But she insisted I needed something lighter for dinner and dancing, and gave me an advance on my salary.

I'd felt quite the lady as I browsed through the racks, even if my mother would have raised her eyebrows. She doesn't think ready-made will catch on, because of the trouble of getting a good fit. But I was pleased with the result: a lilac voile with a fresh, white leaf pattern that draped prettily from waist to just above the ankle. The salesgirl found a matching feathered headband and I felt quite the thing.

Mrs Jameson, in bias-cut apricot crêpe de chine from a Parisian couture house and her usual matching silk turban, was regal elegance personified. She stepped up to the arched front door and knocked.

It was opened by a woman in her early thirties, with bright inquisitive eyes and very straight eyebrows, her soft brown hair falling in waves to just below her ears. She wore the most exquisite earrings of coral and silver, which matched the coral beads and pendant around her neck. Her dress was lovely too: midnight blue silk velvet, with rich coral and turquoise embroidery picking out a pattern that looked foreign – perhaps Indian? She looked exotic, self-possessed, and entirely comfortable.

'Iris, how splendid.' She embraced Mrs Jameson. 'It's been years. Come in. And you must be the famous Marjorie Swallow?'

Goodness. If this was Eileen Power, I needed to revise my opinion of lady academics. I followed them inside, wondering what I'd done to deserve my fame.

Mrs Jameson began to quiz Miss Power about her recent travels in China.

'Simply gorgeous. It was such a wrench to come home,' she said. 'I had almost made my mind up to stay and marry a Chinaman. Now, my rooms are upstairs. Come and meet everybody.'

We went up to a room full of people, noise, and cigarette smoke. Chinese silks hung at the long windows, and a pair of yellow vases with bamboo patterns stood sentinel either side of the fireplace.

'My friends Mrs Iris Jameson and Miss Marjorie Swallow,' called Miss Power into the general hubbub. 'Please come and say hello. Mrs Jameson has just arrived in London and – I hope – plans to settle for a while. Harry, can you get these ladies something to drink?'

A middle-aged man in a crumpled dark suit and sporting a big moustache pushed through the throng. With his spectacles and air of abstraction, he was much more like my idea of an eccentric professor.

'Mrs Jameson, I believe we met once in Oxford?' he asked.

She smiled. 'Mr Tawney. How good to see you again.'

'Now. Whisky and soda, isn't it?' He turned to me. 'What can I get you, Miss Swallow?'

Despite my recent introduction to the delights of The Ritz cocktail bar, I was sensible enough to start slowly. 'A lemonade, please.'

Clutching the glass, I stood next to the fireplace and tried to take it all in. Apart from Mrs Jameson and me, there were eight people present. Mrs Jameson was deep in conversation with Mr Tawney, reminiscing about a golden summer in Oxford before the War. By the door, a sulky-looking young man was talking to a woman who resembled him so much that they had to be related. They stood with a solidly built middle-aged woman in fashionable clothes who seemed somewhat out of place. Perhaps she was their mother.

Silhouetted against the dark window, Miss Power was laughing with a dark-haired young man in pristine evening dress and a very blonde woman in a beaded silver frock. They were both rather beautiful and clearly belonged to the class of people described by the newspapers as Bright Young Things. To my alarm, Miss Power beckoned me over.

'Miss Swallow, I'd like to introduce you to Miss Sarah Simpson and Mr Bertie Post, ornaments of the London stage. Miss Swallow has just been appointed personal secretary to my dear friend Mrs Jameson and has already helped her to solve a murder in record time. Isn't that right? At The Ritz hotel, no less.'

'No! Too thrilling,' said the young woman, opening her sparkling blue eyes wide and clutching my arm. 'Tell all, Miss Swallow. Or may we call you Marjorie? Do call me Sarah, I can't bear formality.'

Laughing, I tried to explain the extraordinary events of my interview with Mrs Jameson in the Palm Court. I was surprised by the immediate jump to Christian names, but perhaps that was how things were done in Bloomsbury.

'Good Lord,' said Mr Post, leaning against the wall in a languid fashion. He was extremely handsome, but I could see by the way he looked at Miss Simpson that his affections were very much engaged. 'So, you're a bit of a Sherlock Holmes, eh?'

I laughed. 'Oh, no. Mrs Jameson is the brains behind the operation,' I said. 'I'm poor old Watson, one step behind and struggling to keep up.'

'Well, Doctor Watson is my favourite,' said Sarah, gaily. 'We'll have to call you Doc. Won't we, Bertie?'

He smoothed his shiny hair. 'I'm playing Sherlock next year, at The Haymarket. You'll have to give me some tips.' He mimed peering through a magnifying glass.

I must have looked confused because Sarah came to my rescue. 'He's an actor. We both are. Don't worry, there's no reason you should know of us. We're not at the cigarette card level of fame just yet. But give us time!'

As if to demonstrate, she pulled out a silver case from her purse and extracted a black cigarette smelling of cloves.

'Darling, would you?'

She fixed the cigarette in a long ebony holder, and puffed it alight as Bertie held a silver lighter to the tip. I watched with fascination. My father smoked a pipe, but thought the habit quite beyond the pale in a woman. I'd never seen a young woman smoke in such an exotic way. Sarah offered the case to me, and I shook my head with a nervous giggle. Who knows what racy habits I might have picked up by the end of the evening?

'Quite right. They stain your fingers yellow – most unattractive. The holder helps, but I've only got the one,' she said. 'Now, tell me all about The Ritz. I've never been yet, would you believe it? I shall have to insist that Bertie takes me. What about the Rivoli Bar? Is it too divine?'

Chapter 3

I was quite disappointed when Miss Power called us all to the dinner table and broke up the conversation. My new friends Bertie and Sarah were seated at one end of the table. Mrs Jameson was nearly opposite me, between Mr Tawney and Miss Power. As I slipped into my place, I heard a snatch of Mr Tawney's conversation:

'So advances in the cultivation of the turnip in Britain were of far more significance to most people than the Wars of the Roses...'

I turned with relief to the man on my right, who had a much less serious air.

'Miss Swallow? I'm Hugh Williams. You're not going to talk about economic history, are you?'

He was about thirty, with a head of chestnut curls, a lilting Welsh voice and an impish smile crinkling his chocolate-brown eyes.

'I shouldn't know where to begin,' I said. And, to show I was as modern as any of them, 'Call me Marjorie.'

'Thank heavens. You work with the American lady, is that right? A detective, from what I hear. We'll have to be careful with our secrets.' Despite his smile, there was a slight edge to his voice. What secrets? I wondered.

'I'm just the secretary,' I said. 'What about you?' His dress seemed almost deliberately negligent: a collar stud missing and his tie loose. His hair was longer than is usual, curling over his soft collar.

'I'm a painting tutor,' he said. 'I work at the Slade School of Fine Art, over in Gower Street. It's part of the University College London, like the history department where Eileen and Harry beaver away.'

'You're an artist?' Perhaps that explained the laxity in matters of collar studs.

'Well,' he paused a moment and poured us white wine from a bottle being passed around the table, 'I used to be an artist. Not a bad one. But I don't think I can call myself that anymore. So, I teach.'

I was pondering how to respond to this, when the fair-haired man who had been by the door took the empty seat to my left. His moustache failed to disguise how very young he was. Eighteen or nineteen, perhaps.

'And this is one of my most promising students, the Honourable Ralph Garrett. Ralph, this is Miss Marjorie Swallow, apprentice detective.'

'How'd you do?' He shot a quick glance at Hugh, who raised an eyebrow. They seemed to exchange a silent message. And Ralph was an Hon, which meant he was the son of a lord, or something. I always got muddled up about that.

'I'm quite interested in art,' I said. It was true; I'd been to the National Gallery many times with Evelyn, and twice to the War Paintings exhibition at the Royal Academy.

'Are you?' The honourable Ralph's dismissive tone verged on rudeness.

Hugh jumped in to cover his student's abrupt answer. 'I'm

glad to hear it. Too many people want to be artists, and not enough to look at art. But Ralph's work is marvellous, especially his landscapes. He has a way of capturing the movement of the skies, the great cloudscapes over the sea. They make me think of Constable and Turner.'

I smiled encouragingly at the young man.

'My people live in Suffolk,' he said. 'I grew up with those skies. But you have to come to London to learn to paint properly.'

The young woman who so resembled him took her seat opposite us, next to Harry Tawney. She was like a paler, older version of her brother, and her dress was truly terrible. It hung on her like a sack, and, despite the good quality of the silk, it was quite the wrong shade of pink for her sallow complexion.

'My sister, Winifred,' said Ralph, stiffly.

I smiled across the table. 'I'm Marjorie Swallow,' I said. 'Your brother was telling me that your family comes from Suffolk. Did you live near the sea?'

She rolled her eyes in an alarming manner. 'Oh! How I love the sea,' she said. 'Such an inspiration. It hurts to be away from it, Miss Swallow. But we needed an escape from Bessborough, and Bloomsbury beckoned. We took a house in Doughty Street, where Charles Dickens once lived. The literary influence, you know.'

'Are you an artist too?' I asked.

'My artistry lies in words. At least, such art as I have accomplished,' she said, looking a little downcast.

'Winifred's writing a novel,' said Hugh.

Now, that was something I had always rather liked the idea of doing myself. 'How exciting! What's it about?' I asked.

She looked at the ceiling. 'It's hard to explain. I want to

capture something of the dreadful transience of our existence, and the invisible currents that flow through our lives, tossing us hither and thither, leaving the merest ripples in our wakes,' she said.

'It sounds lovely,' I said, politely. I'd tried reading that sort of thing before. I preferred detective stories.

The older woman who had been with the siblings earlier sat down heavily between Ralph and Bertie, giving off a waft of cheap lilac scent. She looked around, beaming. She was certainly old enough to be the mother of the siblings, but close up I could see there was no resemblance. Ralph nodded curtly to her and turned away, his face crumpling into a scowl.

'Well, isn't this nice? My favourite young people all together,' she said. Her accent was anything but aristocratic. I recognised elocution lessons when I heard them, having had plenty of them myself. 'And a new friend too, I hope?' She smiled at me. 'I'm Mrs Norris, dear. Betty Norris, in these artistic circles. And you are Marjorie Swallow, is that right?'

Her voice was cosy, her smile inviting. But there was something about her presumed intimacy that set my teeth a little on edge; very different from the casual friendliness of the actors.

'That's right.'

Hugh leaned across. 'Marjorie is helping Mrs Jameson in her sleuthing business, Betty. So we all need to be on our best behaviour.'

I laughed along, but found it rather annoying. No-one would talk to me at all if he kept warning them off.

'How fascinating,' purred Mrs Norris. 'Tell me more about Mrs Jameson. She's American, isn't she? The family's from Boston, I believe.'

I nodded. 'Yes, but she's lived on the Continent for years.' Mrs Jameson had explained once that she sailed across the Atlantic with an aunt who had married an Englishman. She'd travelled all over Europe before settling in Italy.

'So I understand. Rome, wasn't it? And she intends to settle in London, our hostess informs us. What of Mr Jameson? Will her husband be joining her, or is he still in Italy?' She squashed a set of pince-nez onto her little nose and peered at me through small, glittering eyes.

'Mrs Jameson is a widow,' I said.

'Of course. I had forgotten.' She smiled and laid a hand on her amply upholstered breast. 'I too have been alone since my dear Thomas died. I understand how hard it is to make one's way as an unprotected female.'

'I'm sorry to hear that,' I said, feeling uncomfortable at this soul-baring.

'Thomas was a man of the cloth, bless him. Unworldly. I was almost entirely unprovided for on his demise, but I have kept afloat these twenty-five years. One must have friends, Marjorie, if one is to navigate this treacherous world. Tell me more about poor Mrs Jameson. What was her husband's position? Was it a recent passing?'

I set down my wine glass and picked up my knife and fork. Miss Power's housekeeper had served the first course, asparagus in aspic. I was desperate to taste it. Besides, the conversation was not to my liking.

'I haven't the slightest idea. She doesn't talk about him,' I said. It was nothing but the truth; I had never heard Mrs Jameson speak of her husband, although she talked often enough about life in Italy and France. With a little shock, I realised that she never used 'we' when discussing her past.

15

'Did you see the Pablo Picasso exhibition last year?' asked Hugh. 'What do you make of this Cubism business?'

I was grateful for the return to general conversation. Happily, Evelyn and I had attended the exhibition of recent works by the Spanish artist. I'd struggled to understand what he was trying to accomplish with his weird shapes and jagged lines and was keen to hear what a proper artist thought about them.

'I don't think I really understood it. He seems to see things differently from everyone else,' I began.

We were soon deep in discussion, with baffling interjections from Winifred across the table. It surprised me that Ralph took no part in the conversation. He sat in silence, ate nothing, and stared moodily at his plate. A very rude young man, I thought.

Chapter 4

I had just polished off a plate of delicious roast lamb, when Sarah, who had been uncharacteristically quiet throughout the dinner, rose from the table clutching a napkin.

'I'm sorry,' she gasped, and ran from the room. Bertie half-rose and looked anxiously between me and Mrs Norris.

'Perhaps you could…' he said.

Mrs Norris began to gather herself together, a gleam in her eye. I jumped to my feet.

'I'll go after her,' I said. 'Maybe she's feeling unwell.'

Out in the corridor, I knocked and put my head round the bathroom door. Sarah was sitting on the edge of the bath, face hidden in her hands. She looked up in alarm, which changed to relief when she saw it was only me. Her big blue eyes were wet.

'Oh, golly. What an idiot I've made of myself,' she said.

'Of course not. I was worried about you. Do you feel unwell?' I asked.

'I… No, nothing like that. I just couldn't bear it.' She shuddered, a touch theatrically. 'You probably didn't hear. That beastly woman, chatting away to Bertie like an old friend, when I know for a fact that she's never set eyes on him before tonight. A whole load of guff about the blessings of marriage and family life. Ugh.'

I was bewildered. Why should the ravishing Sarah care if a middle-aged matron like Mrs Norris talked to her beau?

'All aimed at me, of course. My God, I wish I'd never met her. I wish she was dead, or I was.' The tears spilled over and made sooty tracks down her cheeks.

She looked inconsolable. I hated to see her upset. Impulsively, I hugged her as one would a crying infant. She clung to me, sobbing, while I rubbed her back. Her scent, lily-of-the-valley, made me think of Mum's favourite soap from Woolworths.

After a minute, she gathered herself together.

'Gosh. I'm so sorry.' She pulled away, tried a wobbly smile. 'Thank you. You're very kind.'

'Don't mention it. Do you mind my asking who Mrs Norris is? I don't understand where she fits in.'

The woman had neither the intellectual heft of the academics in the party, nor the glamour of the actors and artists.

'She's a landlady. Not the cosy type, providing bed and board behind net curtains. The sort that has lots of houses scattered around and screws a good rent out of them,' said Sarah, her voice bitter. 'I was one of her tenants, for a while. So was Hugh. He's still friendly with her, for some reason. I think that's why she was invited tonight. She owns property all over this part of London. Don't be fooled by that poor widow business. She's rolling in it. But it's never enough. Not for her. And she goes on, squeezing and squeezing...'

'How do you mean?'

Sarah stopped talking and blew her nose. She washed her face, brushed her baby-blonde curls, and took out a powder compact.

'I'm sorry, Marjorie. I'm not making much sense. Forget it. I just got upset, and I'm talking nonsense.' With expert fingers, she repaired the damage to her maquillage. 'How do I look? Not too gruesome?'

'Beautiful,' I said, sincerely. 'It looks so natural, too. I'd love to try it, sometime. I've never dared, in case I made myself into a fright.'

She laughed. 'Don't. I'll smudge my eye-black again. Well, we can't very well transform you tonight – it would be too startling. But come over to my flat. I'll show you what a subtle bit of powder and paint can do, if you're clever with it.' She fished in her handbag and brought out a stiff embossed card with silver edging.

'Miss Sarah Simpson, actress comic and tragic. Excellent singing and dancing. Represented by Endell Street Entertainment,' it read.

'Oops. Wrong one.' She fished again and gave me a smaller, plainer card. 'Miss Simpson, 72 Amwell Street, London.'

'I'm over in Clerkenwell. I'll move a bit more central when I've got the necessary,' she said. 'There's a big opportunity coming up next month. Top of the billing, and revues are all the rage right now. There's a part for Bertie, too.'

The smile dropped off her face. 'At least, I hope it'll come off. I'll just have to make sure it does. I can't mess this one up, I really can't.'

Chapter 5

By the time we arrived back at the table, everyone was talking politics, and the glasses of peach syllabub were almost emptied. I set about mine with alacrity, but Sarah pushed hers away.

'If it's liberty you want, then socialism is the only answer,' Mr Tawney was saying. 'Or perhaps you believe in liberty for the few, and wage-slavery for the many?'

Mrs Jameson, far from being offended, smiled benignly. 'I'm in favour of everyone doing exactly what they want to do, with as little interference from the government as possible,' she said. 'But I agree that we should provide welfare support for those who need it, and education for everyone who can benefit from it.'

Miss Power smiled. 'Well, that's a relief. We have agreement on liberty and welfare. Now, help me push back the table and chairs. Bertie, the gramophone is ready for your services.'

Jazz music, it appeared, was another of Miss Power's passions. Bertie rifled through her collection of recordings with admiration and started us off with a brisk number from the Original Dixieland Jazz Band. Miss Power was first on the floor, and I was surprised to see Harry Tawney join her and acquit himself quite creditably. Bertie held out a hand to Sarah, and they twirled away.

Ralph Garrett leaned on the mantelpiece and smoked, looking glum. Hugh joined him and seemed to jolly him up. After a minute, they started to laugh. The transformation of Ralph's features amazed me. He looked happy, relaxed, almost handsome. I wondered what his paintings were like. They must be good for Hugh to overlook his manners and speak so highly of him.

Across the room, I saw Winifred approach Mrs Jameson with determination, presumably to talk earnestly about litera-ture. I wasn't sure she had much in the way of small talk. To my dismay, Mrs Norris then bore down upon me in a cloud of over-sweet lilac and grasped my wrist. I had no wish to be interrogated about Sarah Simpson.

'I do hope poor Sarah wasn't unwell,' she began, looking as if nothing could give her more pleasure than such news. 'Girls like that wear themselves out, and it puts their nerves in a state of excitement.'

'She's quite recovered,' I said. 'She just felt a bit faint.'

I wondered what Mrs Norris had done to deserve Sarah's dislike – apart from charging her rent, of course. Despite not knowing the facts, I found myself firmly in Sarah's camp.

'Was it feminine trouble?' Mrs Norris's little eyes looked avid for detail.

My distaste must have shown in my face, for Hugh crossed the room and came to my rescue.

'Sorry to interrupt, Betty, but this is one of my favourite tunes. Miss Swallow, will you do me the honour?'

With relief, I took his hand and we were soon fox-trotting rapidly around the crowded room to The Tiger Rag. I was delighted to discover that he was an excellent dancer, holding me just close enough and guiding us around without those unfortunate collisions that happen when too many people try to dance in a small space.

'Don't worry about old Betty,' he murmured. 'She's a terrible gossip. Tell me, though, is Sarah all right? She looked so distressed.'

'I think so,' I replied. 'She'd been upset by something Mrs Norris said to Bertie. But they seem happy enough now.'

The couple whirled past, their faces alight with pleasure.

'Ah. Yes, they do, don't they? Lucky them. Now, Marjorie. Tell me something about yourself. Where did you get your passion for art? And what do you really think about the Honourable Winifred's ghastly-sounding novel?'

By the end of the dance, I realised I'd told Hugh half of my life story and knew almost nothing of his.

'Go on, then. Your turn,' I told him.

Hugh had grown up in south Wales, then moved to London 'to seek my fortune'. He had painted with grand ambition and some success before the War. Then he'd had the usual ghastly time of it in Belgium, although he had not been wounded himself.

'Not a scratch on me in the whole four years, which seems awfully unfair given what happened to everyone else,' he said. His tone was light, but his eyes told another story. 'When I got back, I couldn't think of anything I wanted to paint. There didn't seem much point. Old Tonks, the professor I'd studied with before, was sorry for me, I suppose. He offered me a job showing other poor saps how to paint. Now and again, a student comes along who makes it worth the bother.' His eyes sought Ralph again. 'And for the rest, I decided I might as well enjoy myself.' He grinned. 'Another dance? You dance awfully well.'

I looked across the room to where Mrs Jameson stood near the gramophone. Winifred had vanished and she was under siege from Betty Norris. Maybe I should rescue her, as Hugh had rescued me.

'I should see how Mrs Jameson is getting on,' I said, reluctantly. 'I don't know how long she wants to stay.'

'Don't worry about her,' said Hugh. 'I bet your boss is more than a match for Betty. Look, she's sending her packing.'

As we watched, Mrs Norris's face turned a dark red and she backed away sharply, as if she'd been slapped. I couldn't hear what they had said, but Mrs Jameson looked serene as ever, a particularly feline smile on her face.

'Oh, well,' I said. 'Maybe just one more dance.'

Chapter 6

My feet were pinching like mad in my new satin shoes, and my head ached from the heat, the wine, and the noise. I'd danced with Bertie, several times with Hugh, and even with Mr Tawney. The evening had been much more fun than I'd expected, but I wasn't sorry when Mrs Jameson beckoned me over.

'It's past midnight,' she said. 'If I know this lot, they'll be dancing for hours. I'm sorry to drag you away, but I need my sleep.'

'Of course,' I said. 'I hadn't realised it was so late.'

She smiled at me. 'You seem to have enjoyed yourself, despite your anxieties,' she said. 'I'm glad. I like to see people having a good time.'

Contrary to Mrs Jameson's prediction, it looked as if the party was already breaking up. Winifred was gathering up her handbag and gloves, looking very uncomfortable. Mrs Norris was close beside her, one hand on her arm, whispering in her confidential manner. Ralph had been deep in conversation with Hugh when he noticed his sister's plight. He broke off abruptly and grabbed Winifred's arm. Hugh stood back, frowning, as Ralph almost dragged his sister from the room, barely pausing to say farewell to our hostess on the way.

'Dearie me, what a hurry,' said Mrs Norris into the sudden quiet after the gramophone record ended. 'I'd better get along too, Miss Power. It's been such a lovely evening.' She beamed around the company. 'So pleased to make your acquaintance, Mrs Jameson. And you, young Marjorie.' She waggled her fingers at Sarah and Bertie. 'Sweet dreams, my dears.'

'I'll walk you home,' said Hugh.

'Goodness me, there's no need for that, dear boy. It's just a step away,' she said, picking up her fur coat and handbag.

'I don't mind,' he said. 'It's not out of my way.'

'I won't hear of it. I know you, Hugh. The night is young. There's plenty of time for more mischief! Goodnight, one and all.'

She disappeared down the stairs. The entire room seemed to exhale.

'Won't you stay for one more drink?' asked Eileen.

'Another time,' said Mrs Jameson. 'I'm quite exhausted. And the house-hunting begins again tomorrow. I'm not sure I can bear another dreary Belgravia mansion.'

Eileen gave her quick smile. 'Come out this way, that's my advice. We may not be fashionable, but we do have fun.'

Mrs Jameson settled her turban, and I helped her into her mink. 'I can well believe it. We shall talk more, Eileen. Thank you for a most delightful evening.'

Mr Tawney, Sarah, Bertie, Hugh and I followed her down the stairs and into the square. The air was cool against my flushed cheeks. I remembered with glee that Mrs Jameson had insisted I stay the night in a small side-bedroom in her suite at the hotel. How marvellous not to have to run for the last tram going south of the river.

'Let me find you a taxicab,' said Hugh. 'Bertie, you'll see

Sarah home? You're in quite the wrong direction, or we could all share.'

'Rather,' said Bertie, offering Sarah his arm. 'I've got the motor, anyway.'

Sarah kissed me goodbye and made me promise to visit her soon, before hopping into a dashing bright blue Lagonda sports car parked by the kerb. I was rather keen on motors and spent ages looking into the showrooms on Piccadilly, imagining what I would drive if I had money. A Lagonda was high on the list. Bertie cranked the engine, and they roared off towards the Gray's Inn Road.

Harry Tawney walked up the steps of the house next to the one we had just exited. 'This is me,' he said. 'Very convenient. Safe travels, Mrs Jameson. I look forward to further opportunities to convert you to the cause of socialism.'

We walked south to Guilford Street, and Hugh hailed a cab.

'I say, would you mind if I shared with you as far as Piccadilly? I thought I might drop in at the Café Royal. See if any of the usual crowd are still standing.'

We squeezed in and drove off through the quiet streets.

Chapter 7

The moment we had set Hugh down on the pavement at Piccadilly Circus, Mrs Jameson hooted with laughter.

'What an evening!' she said. 'Eileen is right; they certainly know how to enjoy themselves. And plenty of drama swirling below the surface. What had upset Sarah Simpson? That ghastly Norris woman?'

I gazed up at the bright lights of the illuminated signs for Bovril and Schweppes Ginger Ale. The thrill of being out in a taxi at midnight in the heart of London was still new. I looked back to where we had set Hugh down, but he had gone.

'That's right,' I said. 'I didn't understand it, though. She said Mrs Norris had been talking to Bertie about marriage and babies, and that it was aimed at her. Maybe she was implying that Sarah should retire from the stage and settle down.'

'Hmm.' Mrs Jameson yawned, not bothering to cover her mouth with her hand. 'She plays a dangerous game, that woman. She asked me the most impertinent questions. I can't think why Eileen would have her in the house.'

'Sarah said it was because she's a friend of Hugh,' I told her.

'Is she, now? I wonder why Hugh goes along with it. He seems like an independent young man.'

The cab pulled up outside The Ritz. I paid the driver from

Mrs Jameson's purse, and we walked into the hotel. By now I was on friendly terms with Jim the doorman, and even Sidney, the boy at the reception desk, had stopped looking down his nose at my dowdy clothes. Not that there was anything dowdy about me tonight.

'Evening Mrs Jameson, Miss Swallow. Will you be needing anything sent up to your rooms?' he asked.

She thought for a moment. 'I'd like a small glass of brandy, Sid. Marjorie?'

'No, thank you.' I'd had about as much wine as I could manage without it bringing on a headache in the morning.

We took the lift to the suite. I hoped Mrs Jameson wouldn't want to sit up late talking. Now that we were inside, I wanted my bed. Fortunately, she wasn't the type for cosy girl chat in the early hours.

'Your bedroom is through there, Marjorie. There is a shared bathroom in the corridor, second on the left.' She didn't want me using her private bathroom, which led off her sumptuous bedroom. I was quite relieved; it would have been too inhibiting to worry about being overheard.

In the privacy of my room, I took off my shoes and rubbed my sore feet. The bed was soft and twice the size of my narrow little cot at home. The sheets had been turned back and a carafe of water set on the bedside table. Luxury.

After my ablutions, I stretched out in the cool linen, wriggling my toes with delight. I must lie here a moment and enjoy it, I thought.

Instantly, I was asleep.

Chapter 8

I woke with a jolt. Something was making an infernal noise in the next room. It took me a moment to realise where I was, and that the noise was the telephone bell. Answering the telephone was one of my duties.

I jumped up and ran through to the living room, still in my pyjamas. Mrs Jameson liked to sleep late after a night out, she'd informed me. A glance at the clock told me it was not quite seven.

'Mrs Jameson's suite.'

'Oh, I'm glad it's you, Miss Swallow. I was worried about putting the call through so early, but the lady was very insistent.' I'd become friendly with Heidi, the telephone operator at The Ritz.

There was a click, and another voice came on the line.

'Iris? Iris, something dreadful has happened.' The caller's voice was raw with distress.

'This is Marjorie Swallow, Mrs Jameson's secretary,' I said. 'How can I help?'

'Oh, Marjorie. It's Eileen Power. Can you get Iris for me? I'm sorry to call so early, but it is rather urgent. There's been… there's been a death.'

I tapped on Mrs Jameson's door. After a moment it opened.

She wore a floor-length quilted robe in purple satin, buttoned to the neck, and a look of great annoyance. Her nostrils flared and she looked at my striped flannel pyjamas with hauteur.

'Yes?'

'I'm so sorry. Miss Power is on the line, and she says it's urgent,' I relayed.

She swept past me and picked up the receiver. I hovered, desperate to learn more. Who had died? What dreadful thing had happened?

'Eileen… Good Lord. When was she discovered? …Yes, I see. And it was inside the house? Well, then… No, of course. Yes. Yes, I'll see what I can find out.'

There was a pause and she turned to me, miming that she wanted writing materials. I brought her pen and paper, and she scribbled a few words in her large, clear handwriting. I turned my head to read: Norris, two o'clock. Sidmouth Street. Guest list.

'Of course. I will speak to the inspector at once. Leave it with me. And Eileen? I wouldn't telephone anyone else just yet. The police might take a dim view of it. Tipping off the suspects and all that jazz.'

She set the telephone receiver back in its cradle with a grim smile.

'Get out of that ridiculous nightwear and ready yourself for the fray, Marjorie. The Metropolitan Police have been interrogating poor Eileen at Mecklenburgh Square. Mrs Norris was found murdered in the early hours of the morning. It seems we may have been the last people to see her alive. Excepting the killer, of course.'

Another murder! Shocked, I scampered back to my room to dress, remembering guiltily how I had disliked Mrs Norris and shared in the gossip about her. Through the door, I could hear Mrs Jameson pick up the receiver again.

'Heidi? Good morning, dear. Would you please place a call to Scotland Yard, and ask if Inspector Peter Chadwick is available?'

There was a wait of several minutes. When I emerged from my room with hastily brushed hair, buttoning my jacket, she was still standing at the telephone.

'I see… well, perhaps when he is back, you can tell him Mrs Iris Jameson would like to speak to him about the Sidmouth Street murder investigation.'

She replaced the receiver with unnecessary force. I'd already learned that Mrs Jameson did not like to be kept waiting.

'Order breakfast, Marjorie. We may as well fortify ourselves.'

While she bathed and dressed, I cleared the dining table, which was half-covered with details of houses that we had seen, discounted, or were considering. We had two viewing appointments that morning, which I supposed would need to be put off. I checked Mrs Jameson's engagement diary, which was on the desk next to the telephone. There was nothing else today, although she had an appointment to dine with the American Ambassador the next evening.

I opened the door to Graham Hargreaves and an entourage wheeling trolleys and carrying trays. He set out salvers of scrambled eggs, bacon, mushrooms, and kidneys, and laid the table with silverware. Mrs Jameson swept back in, her toilette complete and her earlier irritation smoothed over.

'Excellent. Please pour the tea, Marjorie. I could drink a bath-tub of it this morning.' She lifted the lid on the bacon and piled it onto her plate.

There was a knock on the door and a nervous-looking maid

put her head into the room.

'Sorry to disturb, Madam. There's an Inspector Chadwick downstairs for you.' She held out a silver plate with a pasteboard card, on which showed the insignia of the Metropolitan Police.

'Oh, splendid man. Show him straight up,' said Mrs Jameson. 'I bet he hasn't breakfasted yet. Graham, can you arrange reinforcements? Peter has a healthy appetite, especially when he's investigating a murder.'

Chapter 9

Inspector Chadwick polished off the last of the kidneys, wiping his plate around with a triangle of toast. He stretched out his long legs under the table. His tie was awry, his eyes tired and his chin was shadowed with bristle. He had the air of a man who was all too used to being called from his bed in the middle of the night.

'That hit the spot. Thank you, Iris. Now, pour me another cup and tell me everything about the party last night. That historian woman didn't strike me as the murderous type,' he said.

'That historian woman is one of my greatest friends,' said Mrs Jameson. 'Not to mention a most brilliant thinker. And no, I've never known her to murder anybody, despite much provocation. You will have to tell me what you know in exchange, Peter.'

Graham cleared away the plates while I gathered my writing things and prepared to take notes. Mrs Jameson had made it clear that the role of recording angel would be my primary duty when we had an investigation in hand.

'I'll tell you what I can,' said the Inspector. He eyed my shorthand with suspicion. 'But this goes no further. Understand?'

We both nodded fervently.

'Mrs Elizabeth Norris, widow of this parish, was found dead shortly after two o'clock this morning. There's no sign of a break-in and she had money in her coat pocket, so burglary seems unlikely. Her throat had been cut.'

Her throat! I put my hand to my neck, felt my pulse surge strongly against my fingers. What a brutal thing.

'So, we're assuming it was someone who knew her. The last people we know saw her were at Miss Power's party. Now, over to you. Who was there, and who are they?'

Mrs Jameson listed the people present at the party, and what she knew of them.

'Miss Power and I became friends in Paris, where she was a student at the Sorbonne. Then we met each other again in Boston, a year or two ago. She's always had a knack of gathering an interesting crowd of people – not just academics, but writers, musicians, actors, artists. So last night's guest list was quite typical.'

'Except for Mrs Norris?'

'Indeed.' She turned to me. 'Marjorie, you said she was invited with that artist chap in whose arms you spent half the evening.'

I blushed to the roots of my hair. 'You mean Hugh Williams?' I had a sudden flash of memory and realised I'd been dreaming of him, the two of us twirling around a dance floor while syncopated rhythms played. How embarrassing.

'Don't tease her, Iris.' Inspector Chadwick turned his sharp hazel eyes on me. 'What did you hear, Miss Swallow?'

I thought back. 'Sarah said Mrs Norris was a landlady, and that Hugh had been her tenant. Sarah thought Hugh and Mrs Norris were friendly, and that's why Mrs Norris had been asked along.'

Inspector Chadwick made a note. 'Most interesting. We are already having a chat with Mr Williams, for a number of reasons. Who is Sarah and how did she know all that?'

Oh, goodness. Did that mean Hugh had been arrested? I hoped not.

'Is he under arrest? I'm sure it wasn't him,' I said.

The inspector raised his eyebrows. 'I'll bear that in mind, Miss Swallow. He'll be released as soon as he can account satisfactorily for his movements for the remainder of last night. Now, tell me about Sarah.'

I tried to push away my dismay and answer his questions properly.

'Sarah Simpson. She's an actress. She had also been a tenant, although not anymore. She said Mrs Norris owned property all over the Bloomsbury area of London.' Sarah had also said she wished Mrs Norris was dead, I remembered with disquiet, but we all say things we don't mean.

The Inspector took another corner of toast and smothered it in marmalade.

'Now, tell me how the evening went. Any arguments or rows? Did anyone threaten to punch anyone or burst into tears? I know what these bohemian parties are like.'

Mrs Jameson laughed. 'How worldly you are, Peter. Well, Harry Tawney and I argued a great deal about whether socialism is the future of civilised nations, but we restrained ourselves from physical violence. Winifred Garrett looked like she was going to cry when she described her difficulties finding a publisher for her novel, but I'm rather on the publishers' side there. And her little brother Ralph wore a face as long as January all evening and stomped off at the end in a temper.'

She looked at me and her eyes narrowed. 'Sarah Simpson ran away from the table halfway through dinner. Marjorie, tell us about that.'

I shifted uncomfortably.

'That's the actress?' asked Inspector Chadwick, looking up from his notes.

I gave him a precis of our discussion in the bathroom. As a compromise, I said Sarah had wished she'd never met Mrs Norris. 'But I'm sure it was just talk. I mean, she's ever so nice. She cheered up after that and was quite all right by the time we went home.'

'Home,' said the inspector. 'Indeed. Now, please think carefully about this. I've already asked Miss Power, but it helps to have the details corroborated. In what order did people leave? Who went off with whom? And please tell me the times, as precisely as you can manage.'

'At five minutes past midnight – I checked my wristwatch because I was tired – I called Marjorie and said we should leave,' said Mrs Jameson. 'A minute or two after that, Ralph Garrett left in a hurry, taking Winifred with him.'

Inspector Chadwick paused. 'That's Ralph and Winifred Garrett, the brother and sister of Lord Bessborough? How tiresome. I suppose I'll have Commissioner Groves breathing down my neck until we have our man.'

'Mrs Norris left next. Hugh Williams offered to walk her home, but she said it wasn't necessary,' said Mrs Jameson.

The inspector scribbled. 'So, she left alone?'

Mrs Jameson confirmed that she did. 'She said it was only a few steps away.'

He nodded. 'Perhaps a five or ten minute walk. We don't

yet know which path she took.'

Mrs Jameson continued. 'The rest of us left together shortly afterwards. Harry Tawney wished us goodnight and went into his house, which happens to be next door. Sarah Simpson and Bertie Post, her handsome escort who is also on the stage, jumped in his motor car and went north. Hugh Williams hailed a taxi for us on Guilford Street, going south. We travelled together as far as Piccadilly Circus.'

The inspector stopped writing. 'Wait. You shared a taxi with Hugh Williams? Where did he go?'

'We set him down at the Circus, then the taxi took us along Piccadilly. I didn't see where he went. Did you, Marjorie?'

I hadn't. I'd lost sight of him while looking at the illuminations. 'He said he was going to the Café Royal on Regent Street,' I supplied. 'He was going to see if any of his friends were there.'

Inspector Chadwick scribbled away. 'That's most helpful. Thank you, Miss Swallow.'

'And we got back to The Ritz at about a quarter to one,' said Mrs Jameson. 'No doubt Sidney from the reception desk will be able to tell you more precisely. Now, enough of the interrogation, Peter. What do you know about Mrs Norris?'

He took out his pocket watch and checked the time. 'I can't stop longer. I was on my way to see the murder scene, but when I heard you were involved, I thought I'd stop off and get the background. Not to mention breakfast.' He grinned. 'Sorry.'

Mrs Jameson rose to her feet, eyes gleaming. 'Then we can talk as we go. No, don't protest, Peter. We're going anyway, so you might as well take us with you and pick my brains.'

Chapter 10

The inspector's motor car pulled up outside Eileen Power's house. I looked up at the windows, wondering if Miss Power was watching us. It was a chill, dreary day with clouds that threatened rain.

A young, uniformed policeman, who had been leaning against the garden railings scratching his neck, jumped to attention.

'Morning, Sir. They said you wanted someone to meet you here? I'm Constable Yates.'

'Good morning, Constable,' said Inspector Chadwick. 'Got a stopwatch? I want to time how long it would take Mrs Norris to walk home.' He unfolded a map onto the roof of the car. 'You're from the local station? Good. Show me the quickest way.'

The boy pointed his stubby finger at the map. 'Turn right out of the house, walk up Mecklenburgh Street and turn left onto Heathcote Street, here. Then through to St George's Gardens, following this path. It comes out on Sidmouth Street. The Norris house is number 51, next to the park entrance, here. Otherwise, she'd have to go right down to the Gray's Inn Road and walk around the block.'

'I suppose the park gates are open? Or do they close them

at night?' asked Inspector Chadwick.

'They're usually open. Cause us no end of trouble, what with the…' he glanced at me and Mrs Jameson and revised what he was about to say, 'night-time activities. Nuisance to the neighbours and so on.'

Inspector Chadwick narrowed his eyes. 'But you think a respectable middle-aged woman would have risked going through this park alone, at midnight?'

'Oh, yes. Nothing scared Ma Norris,' said Constable Yates. 'Half of Bloomsbury paid her rent. No-one bilked her. She had it all sewn up.'

'She was known in the neighbourhood? Popular?' asked the inspector.

The constable laughed. 'Not her. She was a mean old cat, if you'll excuse me, ladies. And there are those – like my mother – who still wonder how she got the wherewithal to buy up all them houses when old Reverend Norris died. People were scared of her, and that's the honest truth. Scared of what she knew about them, and what she would do if you couldn't turn up your rent on time.'

'Well,' said Mrs Jameson. 'It sounds as if you will have too many suspects, Peter, not too few. You may be looking for a disgruntled tenant, not one of poor Eileen's dinner party guests.'

'It's possible,' he said. 'We shall see. Please walk at a slow pace, ladies. Mrs Norris was not as tall as you, Mrs Jameson, nor was she as young as you, Miss Swallow. So don't hurry.'

The constable clicked his stopwatch, and we dawdled along the street. The grand stucco-fronted houses of Mecklenburgh Square gave way to smaller and dirtier dwellings as we walked, their dazzling whiteness replaced by sooty London brick.

We turned through the wrought-iron gates into the park. It was a strange place, the conventional ornamental shrubs and winding gravel paths interspersed with old box tombs, and a small chapel of rest. Huge plane trees threw long shadows across the lawns in the early light, their yellow leaves making an unattractive mulch beneath our feet.

'It used to be a graveyard,' said Constable Yates, seeing Mrs Jameson's look of enquiry. 'Took all the bodies from both of the St George's churches. Then it got full up, so they made it into a park about fifty years ago.'

I shivered. How very like London, to make a pleasure-park where bodies lay buried a few feet beneath the earth.

'That's Mrs Norris's house.' Constable Yates pointed at the back of a tall, narrow, grimy-looking building behind the wall on the far side of the park. It was the end of a terrace of houses with small back-gardens. Trees crowded the space to the rear of the building and the windows were shuttered and dark.

We crossed to the path which led out of the park onto Sidmouth Street. Something caught my eye. A little heap of cigarette dog-ends, discarded by the park wall. As if someone had stood there for a long time, waiting and smoking. They could have been there a while, I supposed, but wouldn't the park keeper have swept them away?

'Look,' I said. 'By the wall.'

Inspector Chadwick paused and bent over them. 'You have sharp eyes, Miss Swallow. Well spotted. Constable, make a note. And put one in an envelope. We might need to have the tobacco analysed.'

I was congratulating myself on my detective acuity when a thought struck me. 'If the killer was waiting for Mrs Norris, it couldn't have been any of us, could it? I mean, she left the party straight after Ralph and Winifred, while the rest of us were still inside.'

Inspector Chadwick raised an eyebrow. 'You wouldn't consider joining the force as one of our new women police officers, would you? Very good. But let's not jump to conclusions. It might have been a loafer, pausing on his way home. Or a vagrant with nowhere else to go.'

'Or someone engaging in night-time activities,' said Mrs Jameson, her voice bright. 'A coincidence, then. I thought you didn't believe in coincidences, Peter?'

A look of understanding passed between them. 'I'm prepared to make an exception when it seems the simplest explanation,' he said.

We stood before the house. In a compromise with fashion, it was grubby white stucco on the ground floor, blackened brick on the two storeys above. Railings surrounded the steps down to the basement and a black-and-white tiled path led to the narrow front door, painted a shabby blue. There was a fanlight above the door and an arched window next to it, lace curtains obscuring the lower half. The arches above the first floor sashes had been bricked up.

Another police constable stood at the door. Inspector Chadwick went to talk to him and took a brown envelope, which he put into his briefcase.

I was suddenly nervous. What horrors had happened here? And what were we about to see?

'Is she still...?' I'd seen dead bodies before, of course. Most of us who'd nursed in the War were pretty unshockable. I did not relish this, however.

'I certainly hope so,' said Inspector Chadwick. 'There's no need for you to come in, though. In fact, I'd prefer it if you both

41

stayed outside the house. No sense in confusing the crime scene.'

'Don't be silly. You've already seen how sharp Marjorie is. And how can you use my brain if you don't let me see the body?' Mrs Jameson was in no mood to be put off.

He sighed in exasperation. 'As far as the kitchen door, and no further. I mean it, Iris.'

Chapter 11

We filed into the narrow hallway. The stairs were straight ahead, and a door led off on the right into a mean-looking parlour with old-fashioned furniture. It was cold inside, almost colder than it had been in the street. We paused in the doorway.

A man sat in an armchair by the empty grate, head bowed. He had a pinched face, his unshaven cheeks emphasising hollow eyes. He did not seem to have changed clothes since the night before – his black suit was creased and the shirt cuffs grubby. A dark blue paisley-print scarf, none too clean, was wrapped around his neck. His dark hair was awry, and he held a roll-up cigarette between yellowed fingers. A pile of dog-ends littered the heavy ashtray on the table next to him, and ash was scattered on the rag rug in front of the grate. A cup of tea on the table had grown a skin with sitting.

'All right, Roy? Here's the inspector with some ladies who are going to help,' said Constable Yates. 'We're going to have a look around.'

The man looked up; his eyes narrowed with suspicion.

'Mr Norris? My condolences,' said Inspector Chadwick. 'I will do my utmost to find the person who killed your mother. And then they will face the full penalty of the law.'

The man gave a shrug, as if the law was of little interest to him. 'Can't bring her back, can you?' he said.

'We can't,' agreed the inspector. 'And I'm very sorry. Is there anybody we can ask to sit with you? Any family to inform?'

'No, you're all right. It was just us. Me and Mum.' He stared at the floor again. Poor man; he seemed lost without his mother. It must have been a terrible shock for him. No wonder he looked so seedy.

We continued along the hall and took the narrow stairs down to the basement kitchen. The smell of the butcher's shop rose to meet us. I swallowed hard.

'Stand by the door here,' said Inspector Chadwick. 'I don't want you making footprints.'

The room was dimly lit by the light coming from the area, but I could see a spray of blood up the whitewashed wall. My eyes adapted to the low light.

Mrs Norris was face down on the terracotta tiles between the kitchen range and the stone sink. Her head was twisted to one side. All around, the floor was soaked with blood.

The inspector took a torch from his mackintosh pocket and swept it around, then stepped cautiously across the room and crouched to examine the body.

'Who found her?' asked Mrs Jameson.

'Royston Norris, her son,' said the constable, who seemed to be guarding Mrs Jameson and me. 'He said he got home at two o'clock. Saw the gas light down here and called out to see what his mother was doing. When he got no answer, he thought she must have fallen asleep with the lamp still burning. He came down and saw this.'

'And what is this?' mused Mrs Jameson. 'Marjorie, tell me what you see.'

I took a deep breath. 'She's got her fur coat on. She's lying on her front, and there's an iron kettle upside down on the floor next to her. And blood all around her.'

'Good. So, let's think. She has just arrived home after midnight to a cold, empty house. She keeps her coat on because there's no fire. She comes down to the kitchen, to light a fire and make herself a nice cup of tea before bed. And... what do you think happened next, Peter?' asked Mrs Jameson.

He straightened. 'The doctor's report will tell us more. But it looks like she's been coshed over the back of the head, perhaps to prevent her from making a noise. These house walls are thin. Then her throat was cut as she lay on the floor, rather professionally in my opinion, resulting in this blood spray.' He looked across to the constable. 'I don't suppose you found a knife?'

'No, Sir. We're looking for it.'

'Start with St George's Gardens. Could be anything in the undergrowth,' he said. 'The incision is clean. The knife was extremely sharp. Tell your colleagues to watch their fingers.'

'What can't you see, Marjorie?' asked Mrs Jameson. It was one of the first things she'd taught me to look for – something missing.

'Well, the knife,' I said. I checked around the kitchen for the usual things – saucepans, kettle, fire irons, poker. 'It could have been a kitchen knife. Have you checked the cupboards?'

Inspector Chadwick nodded. 'We'll get Royston Norris to look at those, see if there's anything missing. Not that I suppose he spent much time in the kitchen.'

'What else?' asked Mrs Jameson. She had an expectant look that said I'd missed something. Something that wasn't there.

I looked back at the body. Shoes, hat, gloves were all still in

45

place. Then I realised.

'Where's her handbag?' I asked. I hadn't seen it in the hall, and I couldn't see it on the kitchen table or chair. She'd clutched it close to her all evening at Mecklenburgh Place.

Inspector Chadwick crouched again, reached beneath the body, and drew out the brown calfskin bag.

'Well done.' He stood and picked his way back across the room. Fastidiously, he wiped his shoes on the newspaper around the bottom of the stairs.

We trooped back up. At the top we found our way barred by Royston Norris.

'That's enough, now. I've sent for the undertaker. He'll sort her out. You've had a look and you can't bring her back, so it's time you was off. You're not wanted. And that's her property,' he said, indicating the handbag which the inspector was holding rather awkwardly, as if it was a bomb that might go off. 'So, it's mine, now. I'll have it back, if you don't mind.'

Inspector Chadwick viewed this performance with eyebrows raised. 'I'm afraid that's not your decision, Mr Norris. A crime has been committed, and we need to investigate. We will return the handbag, with its contents, once we've processed it for evidence. The undertaker will wait until we've held a post-mortem examination and determined the cause of death.'

'Bloody obvious, ain't it? Someone cut her bleeding throat!' Norris lunged for the bag.

'Come on, Roy. Don't be a mug,' said Constable Yates. 'You know better than that.' He squeezed past and took the man's arm, drawing him towards the street. 'Let's go next door, eh? Mrs Groombridge will make you a hot cuppa.' He looked back at us. 'Sorry, guv. It's the shock, I expect. I'll get him out of the way.'

Inspector Chadwick nodded his assent as the constable manhandled Norris out of the house.

'Goodness,' I said. 'Do you think he did it?' The dog-ends in the parlour had not escaped my notice, and I couldn't think why else a man would not want his mother's death investigated.

Inspector Chadwick sighed. 'I wouldn't rule it out. He says he came down to the kitchen, saw the body and yelled blue murder. The woman next door – Mrs Groombridge – heard the shouting and sent her husband round. He went to find a policeman. But there was no blood on Norris's hands, face, or clothes. And he'd be covered in the stuff, if he'd done it himself.'

Mrs Jameson was tapping her fingers on her chin, as she often did while she was thinking. 'Unless he cut her throat, went away and cleaned himself up, then came back and yelled as if he'd just got home? Where was he until two in the morning, anyway?'

Inspector Chadwick opened his briefcase and flicked through a pocketbook. 'At a friend's house in Somerstown, he says. The officer who took his statement said Royston is a gambler, and so is the friend. Chances are they were running a spieler, an illegal card game. But we'll find out what time he left.'

He took the brown envelope from his briefcase. 'In the meantime, this is why I wanted to know about your bohemian social engagement, Iris. They found this in Mrs Norris's coat pocket, along with a ten bob note.'

He smoothed out a thick piece of artist's drawing paper, with a pen-and-ink sketch in the middle. It showed a man pulling out his empty trouser pockets, a comic expression on

47

his face. I thought I recognised the jaunty pose.

'I'm broke. There's no more where this came from,' said the script underneath. And it was signed, in big loopy letters: Hugh.

Chapter 12

The sketch was clearly by Hugh Williams. What did the message mean – that he couldn't pay his rent? But he wasn't her tenant anymore, and that was hardly grounds for murder, anyway.

'They found it in her coat pocket?' repeated Mrs Jameson. 'How curious.'

'It's by your artist friend,' said the inspector. 'Which rather made us wonder if he had been involved.'

'But he was with us!' I burst out. 'It couldn't have been him.'

'Not if Mrs Norris was murdered between midnight and half past, certainly.' He looked frustrated. 'I wish we knew more precisely her time of death. The neighbours heard nothing until Royston Norris yelled.'

'She still had her coat on,' I observed. 'So, she must have just arrived home. And it only took us ten minutes to walk from Mecklenburgh Square. You timed us. That means she died at quarter past midnight, and Hugh is innocent.'

Mrs Jameson turned her mocking smile on me. 'Unless she went out again, or went somewhere else before going home, of course. You're very keen to absolve Hugh Williams, Marjorie. You must keep an open mind, however charmingly the suspect dances.'

I blushed and bit my lip.

'But this sketch is most interesting, Peter. Have you asked Mr Williams about it? Does he say it was his?'

'We have. He said it sounded like something he'd done. But he denied he'd given it to Mrs Norris. In fact, he said he drew it for his pupil, the Honourable Ralph Garrett.'

Ralph? I thought of the sulky young man, his rudeness to Mrs Norris and to me. He seemed a far more likely villain.

'And Ralph Garrett gave it to Mrs Norris? Curiouser and curiouser,' said Mrs Jameson. She turned to me. 'Marjorie, what did Mrs Norris ask you about at dinner last night?'

I thought. 'She asked lots of questions about you. About your husband, and Rome. I more or less told her to mind her own business. And then after dinner, she asked about Sarah, and wanted to know if she was sick.'

Mrs Jameson glanced at Inspector Chadwick, an unreadable look, then turned her level grey eyes back to me. 'And remind me again what Sarah said about Mrs Norris?'

'That she wished she'd never met her. That she was rolling in money, but that it was never enough, and she kept squeezing people,' I said.

'Anything else?'

I thought of the body lying cold on the bloodied kitchen floor beneath us, and my conscience smote me. 'That she wished she was dead,' I admitted. 'But I'm sure she didn't mean it.'

'I'll bear that in mind,' said Inspector Chadwick, scribbling in his notepad. 'It would be helpful if you could tell us everything, Miss Swallow. We're not going to jump to conclusions about everything a person says, you know.'

Mrs Jameson had taken the handbag retrieved from under

Mrs Norris's body and was emptying it out. A roll of bank notes. Her gilt-framed pince-nez spectacles. A small black pocketbook with a pencil in the spine, a grubby cotton handkerchief, a collection of dog-eared calling cards and a small bottle of Coty's Le Lilas Pourpre scent. She took out the stopper and I recognised immediately the rather cheap-smelling perfume that had hung around Mrs Norris the previous night.

Mrs Jameson opened the notebook and squinted at the tiny handwriting. 'I can't make this out. Marjorie, your eyes are younger than mine.'

I took it from her. Each page was headed with a date. Beneath were lists of names, with question marks, ticks, or crosses next to them. Some had cryptic notes beside them – 'forged will?' read one. Another said, 'marriage dates' and the one below, mysteriously, just 'street'.

I turned to the last page that had been filled in. It was headed with the previous day's date: Thursday 5 October, 1922. Underneath were the names of everyone at the party, with the same format of ticks, crosses, or question marks.

'Write it down,' said Mrs Jameson, eyes gleaming.

Of the nine names listed, Sarah and Ralph had ticks next to them, but no notes. Hugh's name had a decisive cross, as did Bertie's, Winifred's, and mine. For some reason I found this reassuring. Mrs Jameson and Eileen Power both had question marks, while Harry's name showed a question mark which had been crossed out. Beside Eileen Power's name was the single word: 'China'. The word beside Mrs Jameson's name was 'Husband.'

Chapter 13

'Blackmail,' said Mrs Jameson, briskly. 'She's a blackmailer. Everyone with a tick against their name is already paying up. The people with a cross are not targets.' She smiled at me, with her slightly mocking expression. 'You're off the list, Marjorie. She didn't think you had any skeletons lurking in your closet.'

So was Hugh, I wanted to say, but thought better of it.

'And the question marks?' asked Inspector Chadwick.

'I believe these denote people she planned to target, if she could find out something compromising about them.' They held each other's gaze for a moment. Then he nodded and walked to the window.

'So, all of the people being blackmailed by Mrs Norris are suspects,' he said. 'Including Ralph Garrett and Sarah Simpson.'

'And all the others in the book,' I said. I turned back the pages to the previous dates and wrote down the names with a tick against them.

'True. I suppose we will have to interview them all. Tiresome, but there it is. As you said, Iris, too many suspects. Half of Bloomsbury had reason for wishing Betty Norris dead.'

'But half of Bloomsbury wouldn't be admitted to the Norris house,' said Mrs Jameson. 'You said there was no sign of a break-in.'

'No, that's true. Someone she knew – someone she was blackmailing, perhaps? – came in with her, or knocked on the door when she'd just got in. Maybe they'd talked to her at the party, ran after her and caught her up. They said they had money for her, and she offered to make a cup of tea,' said the Inspector. 'They waited until her back was turned, then...'

I tried to imagine Sarah Simpson creeping across the kitchen with a knife. I couldn't believe that she was involved, despite her passionate dislike of Mrs Norris. Besides, to cut a woman's throat? I thought of the physical violence that would be involved, the mess. I couldn't imagine Sarah doing anything that would ruin her pretty silver dress.

'It's a man's modus operandi,' said the Inspector, as if he could hear my thoughts. 'If you're right about this book, Williams was not being blackmailed. And as you say, he seems to have been out of the frame for the most likely time of death. But he gave this sketch to Ralph Garrett, and according to the book, Garrett was being blackmailed by Norris. I wonder why. Any ideas, Iris?'

She tapped her chin. 'A few. His sister was certainly worried about him. We talked about him for a while after dinner, when she wasn't droning on about her wretched book. Let me investigate further.'

He jumped to his feet. 'There's enough to ask him to assist our inquiries, certainly. I'd better get along to Doughty Street. Pack up that handbag and give it to me.'

She did as he said. 'Suits you,' she twinkled as he held it awkwardly before him. 'Are you sure you don't want me to carry it back to the car for you?'

He laughed. 'Looking like a fat-head now and then is all part of the job. Have a think about Ralph Garrett, will you? Call me if you come up with anything.'

Chapter 14

We left the house and walked back into St George's Gardens. Constable Yates and two of his colleagues were searching through the undergrowth along the wall to the rear of the Norris house.

'Any luck?' asked Mrs Jameson.

One man stood, pushed back his helmet, and gave her a look. 'If we'd found it, we wouldn't still be poking through these here bushes, would we, Madam?'

I smothered a smile. Luckily, Mrs Jameson laughed. 'Well, it's nice to be out in the fresh air,' she said. 'Enjoy your morning.'

We crossed to the far side, choosing to ignore the mutterings of a coarse nature that followed us. Various locals were walking through the park, hurrying on their way to work, or strolling around the flowerbeds, watching the policemen with impersonal curiosity, as if they were exotic animals at the zoological gardens.

It was half-past nine by the time we reached 20 Mecklenburgh Square. The pleasant-faced middle-aged woman who had served dinner the night before admitted us and showed us to the upstairs living room. All traces of last night's party had already been eradicated.

'Can I get you tea or coffee, ladies? Miss Power will be down in five minutes. She's working, and I don't like to interrupt her,' said the housekeeper.

'What a marvellous woman,' mused Mrs Jameson as we sipped our coffee a couple of minutes later. 'Produces wonderful food, clears up afterwards and protects her employer from nuisance callers.'

'Millions of women do that every day,' I said, thinking of my mother. 'It's called being a wife.'

Mrs Jameson laughed. 'Exactly. What every working woman needs.'

'What does every working woman need?' asked Eileen Power, breezing into the room in a scarlet silk robe embroidered with a pattern of gold dragons. She sat on a low chair and pulled the robe around her knees. 'Excuse the get-up; this is my writing outfit.'

'Your marvellous housekeeper,' said Mrs Jameson.

'Hush! Don't let Jessie hear you, or she'll leave for twice the wages. She is much admired by my colleagues. I can't imagine how I would manage without her; I'd have poisoned you all last night.'

Her face fell and there was an awkward silence.

'Anyway. What have you found out?'

Mrs Jameson gave her a carefully edited version of what we had learned from Inspector Chadwick and our visit to the scene of the murder.

'Good heavens, Iris, so you've actually seen the body?' exclaimed Eileen. 'I only asked you to talk to your policeman friend. And Marjorie – you had to see this ghastly scene, too?'

I smiled, trying to look brave. 'It was quite dark,' I said. 'We couldn't see that much. And anyway, I have seen dead bodies before.'

'I'm going to ask you something, Eileen. As a friend, and because the police may ask you later,' said Mrs Jameson, her tone sombre. 'You won't mind?'

'Of course not.' Eileen looked bewildered. 'Ask away.'

'Why did you invite Mrs Norris? Did she have any kind of hold over you?'

Eileen laughed. 'No, of course not. I invited Hugh, and he asked if he could bring her. He said she was interested in meeting new people, and that she already knew Ralph and Sarah. So of course, I said yes. What sort of hold?'

'I wondered if she'd tried to find out about anything you would prefer her not to. About China? Your time there?'

There was a long pause. 'She did seem interested in my travels in the Western Hills. She asked a lot about who I knew in China. I met the boy emperor in the Western Hills, with his Scottish tutor, Mr Johnson. A most interesting man.' Eileen's eyes were wistful.

'I got into China from India by subterfuge, you know. The Khyber Pass was closed to women – quite maddening – by some ridiculous colonial bye-law, so I had to don breeches, bundle up my hair and pretend to be a chap.'

Mrs Jameson laughed. 'I would expect nothing less of you, Eileen. But that would not be enough for her to blackmail you.'

'Blackmail?' Eileen rose to her feet. 'Certainly not. And there was nothing she knew about – there's nothing to know – that would have put me in a compromised situation. What on earth are you talking about? You sound quite mad.'

She looked offended, but I wondered if there was a bit too much emphasis in her denial. She walked to the window and looked out.

'I'm sorry, Eileen,' said Mrs Jameson. 'But it seems likely that Mrs Norris had been blackmailing rather a lot of people, including at least two of the guests attending your party. And I fear she had you – and me, I might add – in her sights.'

Eileen turned from the window. 'Horrid old thing,' she said. 'I thought there was something sinister about her, didn't you? All those insistent questions. Who was she blackmailing?'

There was a knock at the door, and the excellent Jessie reappeared.

'Miss Winifred Garrett for you, Miss Power,' she said. 'She seems quite agitated.'

'Show her up.'

Winifred was so pale as to be almost transparent. Everything about her seemed on the verge of collapse. Her tweed skirt bagged, her stocking had a run, and her mouth trembled. Her hat looked at if she had sat on it accidentally.

'I'm so sorry to trouble you,' she said. 'I couldn't think who else to turn to. Charles is going to be fearfully angry.'

'Charles?' asked Mrs Jameson.

'My elder brother, Lord Bessborough. He said something like this would happen. He was altogether against the idea of us taking a house in Bloomsbury. And now he'll say he's been proven right.'

'Have a seat,' said Eileen. 'Coffee and cakes, Jessie, if you would. Winifred, whatever has happened?'

The young woman took a deep breath. 'The police have been at the house. They've arrested poor Ralph and taken him to the police station.' She quivered on the edge of tears. 'They say it's for murder. Whatever will Charles say?'

Chapter 15

'Arrested him? Good heavens,' said Mrs Jameson. 'That's quick work. What happened? We were talking to the Inspector just half an hour ago.'

Winifred took a sip of coffee.

'They called at the door and asked if Ralph was in. He was still asleep – I don't know what time he got in last night – so I went to call him.'

'Wait,' I said. 'Didn't Ralph go home with you after the party?'

'He saw me home, then he went straight off. He said he was going for a walk, and he wouldn't be told what to do by Charles or anyone. He was in a fearful temper – you must have noticed? Charles sent his man Hudson round yesterday afternoon and I heard Ralph yelling at him. Saying Hudson should mind his own business and he would do what he – what he jolly well pleased.

'Anyway, when we got home, I went to bed and fell asleep about one o'clock. I don't know when Ralph got home. The police asked, but I had to say I didn't know.'

'What happened then, Winifred dear?' Eileen sat on the sofa next to her, passing her cake in an attempt to stem her tears.

'Then Ralph came down looking like something the cat had brought in, and they showed him a bit of paper and asked if it

59

was his, and he said it was, and where had they got it from? He said he'd kept it on his mantelpiece, and it had gone missing.

'They asked where he'd been between midnight and two o'clock this morning, and he said he'd been walking around. They asked if he could tell them where he went and he said it was none of their business, in quite a rude manner, unfortunately.'

'Oh dear,' said Mrs Jameson. 'What else?'

'Then – then they asked if Mrs Norris had been extorting money from him. He said not to be ridiculous.' She covered her face with her hands. 'And then they arrested him, on suspicion of her murder. And the awful thing is, Miss Power, that I think it was true about the blackmail. It's the only thing I can think of that makes sense.'

While Eileen and I attempted to comfort poor Winifred, Mrs Jameson stalked around the room, pausing now and then to trace a pattern on the Turkish rug. Eventually she stopped and pulled up a chair in front of us.

'Winifred, you asked me last night if I could help you with a confidential problem. Was it about this blackmail business?' she asked.

The young woman nodded.

'It was about the money. We both had our allowances paid into the one account and used it to pay the household bills. Charles pays for the house, of course. There should have been more than enough. But there wasn't. A cheque I'd given to Fortnum and Mason wasn't honoured. And Ralph kept saying he'd give me the household money next week, but he never did.

'I talked to the bank. They weren't very helpful at first. The account is in Ralph's name, of course. But one cashier rather took pity on me, when I said all my allowance went into it and I hadn't anything left. She said it had been taken out in cash. A hundred pounds a month, which leaves only twenty for expenses.'

'How long had this been going on?' asked Mrs Jameson.

'Four months.'

'What happened four months ago? When did you first meet Mrs Norris, Winifred?'

She thought. 'It was at the opening of an exhibition of students' work at The Slade, back in June. Hugh Williams, Ralph's tutor, organised it, and several of Ralph's paintings were shown. Mrs Norris was very friendly, gushing about how wonderful Ralph's work was. I thought she was something to do with the school. But I suppose it started after that.'

Mrs Jameson reached out and clasped her hands. 'Winifred, look at me. I will investigate this situation, and if Ralph is innocent, I will make sure he does not hang for Mrs Norris's murder. But I need you to be honest with me. Will you do that?'

Winifred held her gaze. 'I will. I truly don't believe Ralph could kill anyone. He's… he's a gentle boy, really, although he seems ill-tempered at times. That's been the problem, I suppose. He was scared of everyone – Father, Charles, the boys at Eton – until he found he could paint. After Father died, he got up the courage to apply to The Slade, and when he was offered a place, he told Charles he'd already left Oxford, and it was painting or nothing.'

She rubbed her eyes. 'We were so happy here, you know. He had found something he loved, and I could devote myself to my writing. We managed without live-in servants, we did everything ourselves, just a daily woman who comes in to clean. It was like paradise, until this wretched business with the money started.'

That explained the state of their clothes, I thought. People who've been brought up with servants never know how to look after them properly on their own. But I felt sorry for poor Winifred, trying to make a go of it independently. Perhaps we were not so different, despite the gulf of money and breeding between us.

Winifred rose and walked to the fireplace. 'I would like you to take this on, Mrs Jameson. I will tell you everything I can.' She looked embarrassed. 'I will be happy to pay whatever fee you require, although it will have to wait until my allowance comes in next month. Or perhaps Charles will pay, as I'm sure he will want to see Ralph cleared quickly.'

There was a banging at the front door. I looked out of the window. A large, very shiny black Crossley motor car was parked outside. Two men stood before the front door, both wearing dark trilby hats.

Winifred crossed the room to join me.

'Oh, my goodness,' she said. 'It's Charles.'

The tireless Jessie reappeared. 'There's a gentleman downstairs who says he's a Lord and wants to know if Miss Winifred is here,' she said, looking determined. 'I told him I'd find out if it was convenient.'

'Winifred?' asked Eileen. 'What do you want us to say?'

'Oh… yes, of course. I'll need to face him soon enough. Maybe it will be better with you here,' she said.

Jessie trooped out again. Winifred, who had recovered some of her composure while talking about her life with Ralph in Doughty Street, showed signs of going to pieces again. I took her hand and squeezed it. She shot me a look of surprise and pulled her hand away.

Two men stalked into the room. One was tall, square-set, and fair-haired, with pale eyes and a superior air. His dark suit was impeccable, if dull; a gold watch-chain in his waistcoat pocket the only sign of ornamentation. He looked like a better-fed, older version of Ralph. The other was shorter, dark and wiry, with a watchful face. Both men ignored Eileen, Mrs Jameson, and me completely.

'Winifred,' said the fair man. He strode across and grabbed her arm. 'This is what has come of all your bohemian posturing. How did you let this happen? Did you not tell the police who Ralph is?'

Eileen Power rose. 'Winifred is my guest here, and this is my house. Please introduce yourself, Sir, and explain your presence in my drawing room.'

I was impressed by her icy authority and stored the words away for future use.

He turned, with barely suppressed impatience. 'I beg your pardon, Madam. I am Charles, fourth Baron Bessborough, and Winifred is my sister. We have pressing family business to discuss, and when I arrived at her home, I was advised she might be here.'

He turned back to his sister. 'Why did you not telephone me at once?'

'Thank you, Lord Bessborough. I am Professor Power, and this is Mrs Jameson and Miss Swallow,' said Eileen. 'May I ask the name of your companion?'

Lord Bessborough looked fit to be tied. 'This is my manservant, Mr Hudson. We have come to take Winifred home and resolve the unfortunate situation she has allowed our brother to become embroiled in.'

Mrs Jameson rose to her feet. 'Miss Garrett has asked for my help in investigating the matter of Mrs Norris's murder and your brother's arrest. I have agreed to take on the case, with my assistant Miss Swallow. I suggest we sit down and discuss what to do next.'

He looked at her in astonishment.

'She's awfully experienced in these sorts of things, Charles,' said Winifred, nervously. 'She's solved murders before. I thought...'

'I cannot believe you would share our family business with this... American woman.' He brought out the last two words as if they were damning in and of themselves. 'We do not require any of your services, Madam, whatever they may be. I will speak to Commissioner Groves myself this morning and resolve this error.' He headed for the door, Winifred's arm still in his grasp. Her brothers seemed very used to dragging her around.

'Ah, dear Bobby Groves,' purred Mrs Jameson. 'You won't get around him by pulling rank, My Lord. He really is – how would you put it as an Englishman? Most frightfully proper. As Inspector Chadwick told me this morning when we viewed the crime scene, the commissioner has said many times that no-one is above the law of the land. Such a refreshing man.'

Lord Bessborough stopped. His man, who had opened the door, stopped too.

'Perhaps, My Lord, we might have a word with the lady?'

I smiled at the familiar south London vowels. This gentleman's gentleman was no gentleman, I'd put money on it.

Winifred wrested her arm free. 'Please, Charles. Just talk to Mrs Jameson. You want to see Ralph cleared of suspicion, don't you?'

Chapter 16

'You may call on me at my townhouse in Mayfair, when you have something to report, Mrs Jameson,' said Lord Bessborough. 'I need not remind you of the importance of absolute discretion in all matters. Winifred, you are to go down to Suffolk by this afternoon's train. Hudson will see you to the station. Mother is distraught.'

Lord Bessborough and his man departed, taking Winifred with them. Mrs Jameson handed me a cheque for a surprisingly large sum, and Lord Bessborough's elaborate card.

'Take these and put them somewhere sensible, Marjorie. Now, sit at the table with me and help me construct a timeline.'

'A what, Mrs Jameson?' I pulled out my pocketbook and pen, glad to have something to do. The business negotiations had been impressive to watch, but did not advance our aim of solving the crime.

'Timeline. A list of what happened, when. It helps to clarify my thinking, and it shows who we can discount once we establish alibis.'

'Do you need me?' asked Eileen. 'Fascinating as this is, I have work to do this morning. But please make use of this room and ask Jessie for anything you want.'

'Thank you, Eileen. That's most kind. And of course, we

don't want to keep you from your work. More medieval nuns?'

'The European wool trade in the fourteenth century,' said Eileen, briskly. 'Too thrilling.'

Under Mrs Jameson's instruction, I drew a table of four columns. Times, events, people, and their whereabouts. I could see immediately how useful this was in ruling people in or out of our list of suspects.

'Assuming that Mrs Norris was murdered soon after she arrived home from the party, we can rule out only Hugh and Eileen,' said Mrs Jameson. 'Hugh was with us; Eileen and Jessie were clearing away here.'

'But that leaves everyone else!' I exclaimed in dismay. 'And anyway, Bertie was seeing Sarah home, so it couldn't have been her.'

'Unless they acted together. Marjorie, please try to leave your personal likes and dislikes outside of this investigation. They're actors, remember? They're trained to show you what you need to see.'

I bit my lip. She was right, I supposed.

'However,' she added, more kindly, 'the timeline shows only opportunity. We also need means and motive. Now, what drives a person to murder?'

I thought of the novels I'd read. 'Money,' I said. 'Like when someone's going to change their will and disinherit you. Or love, if someone's going to marry someone else. Revenge, after someone's done you wrong.'

Mrs Jameson's smile was gently mocking. 'Money, love, and revenge. Very Jacobean.' She sipped her coffee, and her eyes took on a more thoughtful look. 'Do you know, I'm not so sure about love and revenge?' she said. 'If someone kills for love, I'd say that's not real love, but a desire to exert control.

Although thwarted passion is always a dangerous thing. And I believe revenge is something people talk about when they are angry and hurt, but rarely put into practice.

'Money, greed, I'll grant you. That can certainly bring out the worst in people. But I think the main motive is fear. Fear of losing something, fear of discovery, fear of what the other person will do to you.'

She paused and looked down, her thoughts clearly some way from our investigation. She sounded as if she was speaking from experience. What, I wondered, had Mrs Norris known or found out about Mrs Jameson?

She seemed to give herself a mental shake and took another sip of coffee. 'Blackmail is a clear motive, of course. Money and fear. I think we should assume everyone being blackmailed by Mrs Norris is a primary suspect, until proven otherwise.'

'Including the people not at the party?' I asked, hopefully.

'Including the people not at the party. Let's have a look at your list, Marjorie.'

I'd managed to scribble down four names from Betty Norris's black book: Reginald Clegg, Percy Digby, Herbert Bellamy, and Olive Dupont.

'Let's assume they are all from this part of London. Mrs Norris had property here, so this is where her influence was strongest. Marjorie, how do you find out where someone lives in London?'

I thought. 'You need a street name to find them in the electoral register. If they have a telephone, you could try the directory.'

'Good idea. But that's given me a better one.' Mrs Jameson grasped the telephone receiver. 'I'm sure Eileen won't mind.

Hello, operator? Can you put me through to The Ritz Hotel?'
She handed the receiver to me.

Heidi, the telephone operator at the hotel, was delighted to
help. She quickly found the address of Reginald Clegg, who
had a telephone installed in his residence in Fitzroy Square.

'There are two listings for a Percy Digby,' she said. 'One in
Tottenham Court Road – that's for a chemist shop – and one
for Perivale. Which do you want?'

I asked Mrs Jameson.

'Probably the chemist. But give me both addresses,' she said.
'You never know.'

Heidi's vast knowledge of London, after years attending
to the whims of guests at The Ritz, meant she also had
information about the other two names. Herbert Bellamy was
the vicar of St George the Martyr church in Holborn – one of
the two churches, I remembered, which had buried their dead
in St George's Gardens. And Olive Dupont, Heidi whispered,
ran a venerable brothel in St Pancras, which catered for
specific tastes of gentlemen who had been to public school.

'She must be in her fifties,' she said. 'But we have a few
guests who see her every time they are in London. We usually
describe her as a therapeutic masseuse.'

I replaced the receiver, shocked that guests of The Ritz had
such appetites, and that the lovely staff had to accommodate
their requests. We looked at our list of primary suspects with
motive and opportunity.

'Ralph is being questioned by the police. We will have to
find a way to speak further with his sister, to find out what
Mrs Norris knew about him. I'm inclined to believe Winifred.
That boy doesn't strike me as a murderer. But we shall see.

'There's Sarah Simpson – bother! We forgot to ask Heidi for

her address.' Mrs Jameson reached for the telephone again.

'No need.' I took Sarah's card from my handbag. 'She gave it to me last night and invited me to visit. Why don't I go and talk to her?'

Mrs Jameson gave me a long look. 'Yes, you do that. She's more likely to open up to you. Find out what Mrs Norris had on her. Ask her exactly what time she got home, and whether she has any witnesses to her arrival. Don't let her charm cloud your judgement, Marjorie.'

She looked at her wristwatch. 'It's half-past eleven. I'll start with Percy Digby's chemist shop. Let's meet in an hour and a half in Charlotte Street, for luncheon. It's close by Tottenham Court Road. Café Conté, a delightful French place I used to frequent, if it's still open. Take a taxi and see what you can find out.'

Chapter 17

The house in Amwell Street was next to a fried fish shop. A smell of rancid fat hung about the place. It was far from the fancy residence I'd been imagining for a glamorous young actress. Sarah too looked a lot more ordinary without powder and paint, or a pretty frock.

'Oh! Marjorie, what a surprise,' she said, pulling a faded floral wrap around her and tying the sash more tightly. Her lovely blonde hair was tied up in a pink chiffon scarf. She didn't look that pleased to see me. 'Have you heard about this ghastly business with Betty Norris? Come in. I was just about to make some tea. My room's on the first floor.'

I followed her up the narrow stairs. We went into a tiny kitchen that smelled of kippers. Rows of stockings and flimsy underwear hung on the fender. Sarah pushed them aside and reached for the kettle.

'Squeeze yourself through there and sit at the table. You can put those scripts on the floor,' she said. 'Sorry it's such a mess. My room-mate isn't up yet. She's got a matinee, so she sleeps in till lunchtime. Now, let me just find some cups and saucers.'

There were dirty dishes in the sink, and damp patches on the walls. Sarah's attempts at hospitality in these circumstances touched me.

'Here,' I said. 'Let me get those dishes done.'

She began to protest.

'Don't be daft,' I said. 'I'm not a lady. My dad's a draper, down in Catford. I was a VAD nurse in the War. A bit of washing-up doesn't hurt me.'

She grinned. 'One of my first jobs was at the Lewisham Apollo,' she said. 'I played a fairy in the pantomime. I'm not a lady, either. My dad kept a tobacconist shop in Shoreditch. Hold on a minute, let me see if I can get this hot water boiler going.'

It was easier to talk after that, as I washed the dishes, and she cleared away the laundry.

'I can't believe she's really dead,' said Sarah. 'Isn't it dreadful? And to think we saw her just last night. It gives me the shivers. I suppose it must have been a robbery. If only she'd let Hugh walk her home, like he usually does.'

'Actually,' I said, 'the police don't think it's a robbery. They think it was deliberate, by someone she knew.'

'Surely not.' She looked at me sideways. 'How do you know?'

I shrugged. 'I told you Mrs Jameson's a private detective. She rang the policeman in charge, just as soon as Eileen Power told us.'

Sarah twisted the tea-towel in her hands. 'I know I said some awful things about her last night. Mrs Norris, I mean. But it was just talk.'

'I know,' I said. 'We all say things we don't mean. You were upset.'

'The police came round here this morning,' she said. 'Nine o'clock, before I was dressed. Gave me such a shock. They wanted to know what time I got home last night.'

I nodded encouragingly.

'Bertie dropped me off in the Lagonda. It can't have been later than half-past twelve, because he drives rather fast. He loves that car. It's a nippy little thing.' She smiled fondly.

'Well, that's all right then,' I said. 'Was your room-mate in when you got home?'

'Oh, yes,' she said. 'Molly's in a show, so she'd only just got home. We had a cup of cocoa together. We were both dog-tired, so we didn't stay up long.'

Good. We could cross Sarah off the list.

She made tea, apologising for the lack of sugar. 'I hope you don't mind it as it comes. Things are a bit tight right now, to be honest. I'm running low on funds. It'll be better next month when the new show goes into rehearsals.'

I wondered how she managed to keep up the payments to Mrs Norris if she was out of work. Time to try to find out why she was paying her.

'Last night, when you were talking about Mrs Norris,' I ventured, 'you said she was your landlady. Does she own this place, then?'

'Oh, golly, no. I moved away from her as soon as I could,' said Sarah. 'At least a year ago, I should think. It was – it wasn't a very nice place. Just a room in a boarding house, you know? People coming and going all the time. This is much nicer, sharing with a friend.'

'But you said she kept – what was it? She kept on squeezing you. In what way?'

Sarah's mouth hardened into a thin line. 'Forget what I said. I was just upset. Talking a lot of nonsense.' She sipped her tea and looked out of the window.

'I mean, she could be really chummy one minute, like she was your best friend. Then she'd use what you'd told her, turn

72

it against you. And she kept her claws in even if you tried to shake her off, so that you had to say hello and be nice to her at parties and so on. And she was fearfully vulgar – didn't you think so?'

She was, although that wasn't cause for murder. 'But you said she was saying things to Bertie, and that they were aimed at you?'

She smiled, a brittle smile that looked as if she was losing patience with my questions. 'Well, that's the sort of horrible thing she'd do. Make nasty insinuations about a person. What is this – an interrogation?'

The door opened and a young woman in a dressing gown and curl papers pushed through, yawning. 'Hullo. I need some breakfast. What time did you get in, Sarah?'

'Oh – Molly, this is Marjorie. And you know, don't you?' Sarah's cheeks were bright pink and her eyes wide open, as if trying to signal something to her friend. 'Bertie dropped me off at half past midnight and we had cocoa before bed. You must be half-asleep still.'

The girl looked confused, then let out a bright laugh. 'Of course. I'm so sleepy, that's all. I'd quite forgotten.'

She turned to me and held out a hand. 'Pleased to meet you, Marjorie. Excuse my muddle. I'm doing two shows a day at the Palladium and I'm that tired, I can't remember whether I'm Martha or Arthur. Are you in the business?'

'Marjorie's a private detective. We met at last night's party,' said Sarah. 'She just popped round to ask me some questions, but I think she's finished now.'

I left soon after and walked down Amwell Street in search of a taxi, feeling uneasy. Did Sarah really get home at half past twelve last night? And if not, where did she go?

Chapter 18

The Café Conté looked like the sort of Parisian café you see in Impressionist paintings. It had big plate glass windows, a green-and-white striped awning, and little round tables with marble tops. There were tables set on the pavement, but in this chilly weather, no-one was brave enough to sit outside.

Through the glass, I could see a group of men in their twenties drinking glasses of beer, talking with excitement about something and roaring with laughter. But there were women in there too; a few couples scattered around drinking glasses of wine and concentrating on their food. I couldn't see Mrs Jameson.

Oh, well. I squared my shoulders and approached the door. It was immediately swung open by a waiter with a long white apron tied over his black waistcoat and white shirt. I didn't much like the way his dark eyes travelled over me, from my face to my shoes and slowly back up.

He seated me at a tiny table right in the window, as if I was part of the display. But his whole demeanour changed when Mrs Jameson stepped in a few minutes later.

'*Chère Madame, enfin vous etês de retour*! Come this way, please. What a pleasure to see you again. *Venez avec moi, s'il vous plaît.*' He pointed to a circular table in the middle of the room, under a green-shaded pendulum lamp.

'Hello, Artur. Good to be back. I'm joining my assistant, Miss Swallow. I see she is here already.'

I watched as the waiter's face demonstrated rapid adjustments to his previous assessment of me.

'*Merveilleux, mesdames*. Please, Miss Swallow, won't you move to this table?'

I picked up my belongings. Swiftly, a second waiter appeared to take and hang up my coat.

'Now, this is nice,' said Mrs Jameson. 'I haven't been here for years. Let's order first, then we can compare notes. What do you fancy?'

I picked up the menu card and tried to remember my schoolgirl French.

'Garlic snails? Frog's legs?' she asked. 'Carafe of Beaujolais?'

I scanned the menu anxiously, looking for something familiar.

'An omelette,' I said, with relief. 'And some water, please.'

'Two *omelettes aux fines herbes*, Artur, with bread and a *salade verte* to share,' said Mrs Jameson. 'Excellent choice, Marjorie. Although the snails really are very good.'

I decided to take her word for it. A carafe of water arrived swiftly, along with a basket of sliced rounds of French bread, warm and crispy on the outside, and smelling delicious.

'Now, Sarah Simpson. What did you find out?'

'She says Bertie dropped her off at half-past midnight at her rooms in Amwell Street. But there was something odd about it,' I admitted. 'She shares with an actress friend, who was still in bed when I arrived. But she got up for breakfast and asked what time Sarah got home this morning. Sarah had already told me they'd had cocoa together after Bertie dropped her off. So that was peculiar.'

I paused. I hated to say it, but I had to.

'I think Sarah was lying. She said Molly must have been tireder than she realised if she couldn't remember her coming in. Molly looked confused, then seemed to realise something, and she said she'd forgotten.'

Mrs Jameson chewed thoughtfully. 'Something's wrong there, then. Did you have a chance to ask her about Mrs Norris and blackmail?'

'I tried, but she was getting suspicious. She accused me of interrogating her. But she did say that Mrs Norris used to pretend to be all friendly, then use your secrets against you.'

Was that what I was doing? I'd gone there trying to find out about her alibi and whether she was being blackmailed. And now I was telling everything to Mrs Jameson. But then Sarah hadn't told me any secrets. That was the problem.

'Sarah said she got away as soon as she could leave the room she rented from Mrs Norris, but that the woman kept her claws in. She said she didn't like having to talk to her at parties, that she was vulgar.'

Mrs Jameson let out a hoot of laughter. 'Well, that's the worst crime you can commit in England, I suppose. If an out-of-work actress thinks you're vulgar, you really must be beyond the pale.'

We were interrupted by the waiter with two beautifully presented golden omelettes, glistening with butter, and flecked with freshly chopped green herbs. My mouth started to water.

'Bon appetite! Café Conté make the best omelettes this side of the English Channel,' said Mrs Jameson.

As I tucked in, she told me about her adventures with Percy Digby in Tottenham Court Road.

'Mrs Digby was behind the counter. She seemed a sensible woman, quite cosy and maternal. I asked if I could consult her husband about gastric trouble. She said I was lucky because he often had to travel on business, but was in the shop today. She showed me to the back parlour.

'He was the most ordinary-looking little man. Quite small, with a toothbrush moustache and a pair of cheap, wire-rimmed spectacles. I told him I get heartburn after eating late, and he started to make up some powders. Then I asked if he knew a friend of mine who dropped by here sometimes, Mrs Betty Norris.

'Well, bicarbonate of soda went everywhere. While he was apologising and trying to dust me down, I told him she'd been murdered. He went very white, then very red, and asked if it was really true. Then he said he didn't know her, exactly, but that she might be a friend of his wife.'

Mrs Jameson stopped and gave a mischievous grin. 'Which seems unlikely. He was in such a state, I just asked him straight out where he was last night if he'd not heard the news until now. And he said he'd been upstairs at home with Mrs Digby; that their youngest had colic, so Mrs Digby's mother had been staying with them to help and the whole family spent an anxious night awake while the child bawled its head off.

'That sounded like the sort of alibi that was likely to stand up, and I really don't think he'd heard about Mrs Norris's death until I told him. I paid for the indigestion remedy and was on my way out when I mentioned that the telephone directory showed another Percy Digby, in Perivale, and asked did they often get each other's phone calls?'

She smiled again, the cat-smile that showed she'd found something out.

77

'This, apparently, was even more upsetting than my mention of Mrs Norris. He almost pushed me out of the door, followed me and closed it behind him, looking terrified. He said that if I wanted paying, I should come back when Mrs Digby wasn't there. I assured him I was not in need of money. He said it had all got very complicated, and he'd meant to sort out the situation in Perivale, but never quite managed it, and asked if I would be kind enough to say nothing more about it.'

After that, Mrs Jameson had made her way to the public library. 'I looked in the electoral registers. There are two people registered to vote in both Tottenham Court Road and Perivale. Mr and Mrs Percy Digby, at both addresses. Hurrah for women's suffrage, that's all I can say.'

I stared at her. 'He's married to both of them? A bigamist?'

She laughed and picked up her knife and fork. 'You'd think he would be some Rudolph Valentino type, wouldn't you? The Sheik, with his harem of odalisques. But he was just this terrified little man who looked as if he'd struggle to attract one wife, never mind two. There's nothing so mysterious as someone else's married life, Marjorie.'

As she ate, I remembered the word written next to Mrs Jameson's own name, in Mrs Norris's black book.

I rounded off the meal with a luxurious dish of crème caramel while Mrs Jameson imbibed a thimbleful of very dark, very thick coffee, which she pronounced excellent.

'So, let's have another look at the list,' she said. I produced it from my handbag.

'Sarah Simpson, still on the list. Percy Digby, off the list for now. Reginald Clegg, the Reverend Herbert Bellamy, and the redoubtable Olive Dupont. I think Mr Clegg next, don't you?' she asked.

'Wait.' I looked at the name again. 'That's it. I remember now. It was in the newspapers. My mother got very excited about it.' The Clegg affair had been one of the few things my mother had taken interest in since my brother's death. The misfortunes and misdemeanours of others did cheer her up.

I racked my memory for the details. 'Mum noticed because he's in the trade. Clegg and Co is a wholesaler, supplying drapers and outfitters. We bought from them occasionally, although they weren't our main supplier. Then, in the War, they switched to uniforms. There was some trouble about quality, and they almost went bust after the Armistice.

'Then there was a boating accident at Richmond-on-Thames. Reginald Clegg was out rowing on the river with his wife Moira, last summer. They'd only been married two years. Somehow, the boat got upset, and they both fell into the water. He managed to swim to the riverbank, but she got caught up in the weeds, with her long skirt and coat. She drowned, and he was in the paper saying how terribly upset he was and that it was a tragedy and warning people against taking boats out if they couldn't swim.'

I took a breath. 'Then, just four months later, he married her sister. And it turns out that the older sister – that's his first wife – had all this money tied up in a trust from her godfather, which of course Clegg inherited on her death. Clegg and Co survived and are doing very nicely now. Well, like my mother said, you couldn't prove anything, but it didn't half smell fishy.'

Mrs Jameson burst out laughing. 'I expect it didn't half did,' she said, her American drawl more pronounced than usual. 'What a turn of phrase.'

I cringed. I'd let my enthusiasm for the story run away with me and my south London pronunciation had escaped. What would my old headmistress have said?

'I'm sorry, Mrs Jameson.' I blushed to my hair roots.

'Nonsense. I don't need you to put on airs and graces, Marjorie. I like to hear you talk naturally.'

Maybe. But I'd keep an eye on my language from now on.

'Anyway, that is all most interesting. And I can see why it might have caught Mrs Norris's attention. I wonder what she had over them. It's a dangerous business, blackmailing a murderer.'

Money and passion, I thought. Two good motives for murder. And with Mrs Norris, you could add a third. Fear of discovery.

Chapter 19

The house in Fitzroy Square was grander than I'd expected, an imposing front of white stone adorned with all manner of pillars and arches. A maidservant in a black and white uniform asked us to wait in the hall while she went to see if Mr and Mrs Clegg were at home.

We stood on the inevitable chequerboard tiles, such a bother to keep clean of dust and mud from visitors' shoes. A central staircase of gleaming mahogany led grandly up to a gallery. Bad oil-paintings of simpering women in crinolines holding small dogs, and men with big dogs holding dead grouse, looked down on us.

'Please come this way,' said the maid, reappearing. She flung open a pair of white-and-gilt doors to reveal a big room with French windows onto the garden.

Mr and Mrs Clegg had arranged themselves in an impression of domestic bliss and industry. Mr Clegg sat in his shirtsleeves at a small writing desk, surrounded by paperwork. He had a fountain pen in his hand and was frowning over a letter. He looked up, smiled, and laid down his pen.

His wife sat on a chaise longue, an embroidery circle in her hands. Her little feet were raised, and I could see by the loose cut of her afternoon dress that she was with child. She was extremely pretty, the fringed pale-blue shawl around her shoulders accentuating her blonde curls and china-blue eyes. She reminded me a little of Sarah, but without the actress's blowsy warmth.

'Welcome,' said Mr Clegg, standing. He was not tall, but his suit was well-cut and elongated his frame. He had dark, roguish eyes and a rather sensual full mouth. 'I have heard of you, of course, Mrs Jameson. It's a pleasure to make your acquaintance. And this is?'

He looked at me frankly, and I found myself growing uncomfortable. There was something about the man that made me want to blush, stammer, and run back to the school room. Even his voice, deep and melodious, but with something of an edge. You would not want to get on the wrong side of this man. I was glad Mrs Jameson was doing the talking.

'This is my secretary, Miss Swallow,' said Mrs Jameson. 'We have been engaged to investigate a murder, Mr Clegg.'

I watched his face. His smile of welcome did not flicker.

'Indeed? How very dramatic. Do have a seat, won't you?' He gestured towards a little sofa opposite Mrs Clegg.

'Will you have some tea?' she asked in a high, girlish voice. 'Thirsty work, I should imagine. Murder.'

She smiled, her little pearly teeth glinting. A shudder ran down from the nape of my neck to the back of my knees. Hastily, I sat. Mrs Jameson joined me, almost bouncing me off the sofa.

'That would be kind. Forgive me for not making an appointment ahead of time,' she said. 'We are speaking to all known associates of the deceased, and there are many. Can you tell me about your relationship to Mrs Elizabeth Norris, of Sidmouth Street in Bloomsbury?'

Again, Mr Clegg showed no sign of perturbation. He sat next to his wife.

'I saw in the late edition of *The Times* that she'd been bumped off,' he said. 'Perfectly dreadful. Lydia, darling, Betty Norris was your acquaintance, wasn't she?'

Mrs Clegg laid down her embroidery. 'She was my landlady,' she explained, leaning towards us with a confiding smile. 'I rented rooms from her in Holborn before my marriage. We weren't close, but she was good at staying in touch with people. She came to our wedding, bless her. Too kind.'

The tea arrived and Mrs Clegg poured. Remembering the poisoning at the Palm Court, I felt suddenly anxious about drinking it. I set my cup and saucer down.

'And what about your sister's funeral, a few months previously?' asked Mrs Jameson, her voice pleasant and conversational. 'Did Mrs Norris come to that?'

The couple exchanged a glance.

'I don't believe so,' said Lydia Clegg. 'I don't think Betty ever met my sister.'

Mrs Jameson said that the best way to get people to say something they didn't want to say – especially English people – was to leave such a long pause that they found themselves telling you, just to fill the gap. The pause extended into its second minute. Reginald and Lydia Clegg sat in silence, smiling at us with absolute serenity. That, more than anything else they could have done, convinced me of their guilt. No innocent person could have stood it.

Mrs Jameson rose and walked to the mantelpiece, beaten.

'Is this your sister, Mrs Clegg? And your late wife, of course, Mr Clegg.'

She examined a large photograph of a rather dreamy-looking woman in pearls and a low-necked gown.

'That's Moira,' said Mr Clegg. 'We like to keep her there, looking over us.' His tone might have been intended to be wistful, but it sounded simply mocking.

'Lydia and I barely knew each other before Moira's death, Mrs Jameson. Only our shared grief for my late wife drew us together. And as you can see, our present happiness owes much to Moira.'

The shivers were running down my neck again. Their present happiness owed everything to his murdered wife.

'How's business down on Great Portland Street?' I asked. 'Clegg and Co used to supply my parents' shop. But I heard you were in trouble. Weren't you being sued by the War Office over those duff uniforms?'

Mr Clegg turned his rather devastating smile on me. 'Your parents have nothing to worry about, I can assure you, Miss Swallow. Clegg and Co is on a perfectly firm financial footing. We settled with the War Office after an unfortunate misunderstanding about the weight of cloth they required.'

Yes, I thought. You settled out of court, with your wife's trust fund.

Mrs Jameson's nostrils flared; a sure sign she was growing impatient. 'Would you mind telling me where you were last night, Mr Clegg? Between the hours of midnight and two o'clock?' she asked.

He raised his eyebrows, but his face retained its pleasant expression.

'Of course. Mrs Clegg has been rather delicate in recent months, due to her happy condition. But in this last week she has been feeling much better, so we celebrated with a night out. We went with friends to the Lyric Theatre. We took a box, then afterwards we had a late supper together at the Criterion. The Italian Roof Gardens, don't you know? I think we were there until at least two. That dancing girl did two sets, didn't she, darling?'

'Edna Maud. She did. She was terribly good. So was the band.' The little pearly teeth were on display again. I imagined them nibbling away at her sister's marriage, her brother-in-law's morals. If he had any. 'I was so tired, but I could see how much you were enjoying it, Reggie. We stayed until after the second set, then took a taxi home. That's why I'm so sleepy today.' She yawned, her pink tongue curling delicately like a cat, stretching out her creamy limbs. Pearl bracelets adorned both her wrists. I glanced at the photograph of her sister and wondered if those were Moira's pearls, cannibalised for Lydia's jewellery box.

'Thank you. Marjorie, have you made a note of that?' asked Mrs Jameson. With a start, I scribbled down times and dates. Lyric Theatre. Italian Roof Gardens. Unfortunately, it sounded like a watertight alibi, all played out in public.

I tried not to feel envious. The Italian Roof Gardens had opened two years ago and was quite the most fashionable place in London. I'd only read about it in newspapers – an Italian-style garden with artificial starry skies, musicians to serenade you over supper, and dancing until all hours.

A handsome, rich husband, a glamorous life, beauty, and a baby on the way. Lydia Clegg had it all. But was she happy? I glanced at her smiling face. Yes, I conceded. Yes, she was.

'You've been very helpful, Mr and Mrs Clegg. We will, of course, ensure that your alibi holds. Can you give me the names of the friends you spent the evening with?'

Mr Clegg laughed. 'I can see you take this very seriously,

Mrs Jameson. Here's my friend's card. He'll vouch for me, as should the waiter at the Roof Gardens, given the size of the tip I gave him.'

'And the play you saw at the theatre?' I asked. I'd read a detective novel where the murderer was caught because he hadn't seen the last act of the play he'd said he was watching, so didn't know the ending.

Lydia Clegg smiled at me. 'It's a new comedy,' she said. 'Terribly good; you should go. It's called *How to Get Away with Murder*. And you have to wait until right at the end to find out if they do. I'm sure you'd find it amusing.'

Chapter 20

'Terribly amusing,' said Mrs Jameson, her voice bitter, as the door shut behind us. 'Aren't they ghastly? They've faced down the inquest, so I suppose they feel safe enough to laugh at us, Marjorie. And that was a suspiciously complete alibi, don't you think? If there's so much as a chink in it, I'll find it.'

I hoped that might involve a trip to talk to the waiting staff at the Roof Gardens. Even my mother would be interested to hear about that, not to mention Evelyn. She'd said the social scene in Cambridge was hopelessly dreary, especially for women. Lots of drinking cocoa and sitting up late talking, but not much dancing and jazz.

'If they were safe, why would Mrs Norris be able to blackmail them?' I wondered.

Mrs Jameson stopped. 'That is an excellent question. Or are they feeling safe this morning because she is dead? Let us think. Mrs Norris was Lydia Clegg's landlady. Which fits with what you told me about Sarah, I suppose.'

Sarah. I still hoped there was an innocent explanation for Molly's confusion about her return home. I wished I had pressed my questions more strongly. Perhaps I should go back and talk to her again.

'Clegg said that they hardly knew each other before his wife died,' Mrs Jameson observed. 'But what if Mrs Norris knew that he used to visit Lydia at her lodgings, while still married to Moira? That would rather undermine his story that they fell in love after Moira's death.'

What was it Sarah said? Betty Norris pretended to be your friend and then turned on you. I could just imagine her, the sympathetic and discreet landlady, turning a blind eye to the handsome man visiting her pretty young lodger.

'I bet she kept notes, don't you?' said Mrs Jameson. 'All of his comings and goings, the dates and times. Then – when the sister is safely buried, and the murderous couple are married – she pounces. The secret visits stay secret; the money is paid monthly. Out of poor Moira Clegg's trust fund.'

She stood by the edge of the road. Fitzroy Square had a pleasing design: a circular garden in the centre within a square of houses, a road around the inside of the houses.

'We need to find those notes,' said Mrs Jameson. 'We found the pocketbook she takes about with her. But she must have a dossier or ledger somewhere at home. Proof of all the skeletons in the cupboards. We must know what she knew.'

As we talked, a plain-looking black motor car with white-walled rubber tyres travelled slowly around the square, as if the driver were looking for a house number. At first, I thought it was a taxicab, but it bore no advertisement for hire. The driver was muffled up in a scarf, his hat pulled low, barely visible behind the glass windscreen.

Mrs Jameson stepped into the road, towards the central garden. 'I'll ask Peter if he's found anything. If not, maybe we should go back and search the house for it,' she said.

We were in the middle of the road when I noticed the car make a second circuit of the square. I began to feel uneasy.

'Look at that motor,' I said.

It sped up, clipping the inside corner of the road as the engine roared into top gear. I screamed as the car hurtled straight for us. Mrs Jameson looked around. I ran towards the garden, then realised she was frozen with shock.

'Come on,' I shouted, running back into the street and grabbing her arm. The heat of the motor scorched my face and I smelled hot oil and engine fumes. I pulled urgently at Mrs Jameson's coat sleeve and she stumbled after me as the driver swerved towards us. We were almost at the garden when the car hit her. She cried out and we both fell to the ground.

I landed hard on my hands and knees in the gravel. The car stopped ten or twenty yards on. Perhaps it had been an accident, although it had felt deliberate. Then I heard the clanking of gears. The driver was putting it into reverse.

'Get up!' I shouted. Mrs Jameson lay beside me, unmoving. Her eyes were closed, her face very pale. For a dreadful second, I thought she was dead. Then she moaned, and her eyelids quivered.

The car was coming back. I scrambled to my feet, put my hands under her arms and heaved. There was a bench almost next to us. I pulled her unyielding weight behind the cast-iron bench, crouched next to her, and prayed.

I heard shouting and a police whistle. The car, which had been barrelling towards us, stopped. The driver changed gears again and pulled the wheel around sharply. The car veered towards the side street at the next corner of the square.

It screeched away. I looked for a number-plate, but it had been removed.

Mrs Jameson was still ghastly pale, her shallow breath coming in gasps. It was shocking to see my usually composed employer lying on the street, her hat off and her elegant gaberdine coat pulled up around her knees. I tried to straighten it out. As I did so, I noticed her foot was twisted at an awkward angle.

'Mrs Jameson? Can you hear me?'

Her eyelids quivered. She opened them for a second, then let them fall.

I looked in desperation for help. Three people were running towards me. The first was the housemaid who had answered the door at the Cleggs' mansion. Behind her was a working man in overalls and cloth cap, and a policeman, buttons gleaming, who blew his whistle as he ran.

You can stop your noise, I thought. We're not going anywhere.

'Oh, Miss! I saw it happen from the parlour window,' said the girl. 'Is she dead? They shouldn't be allowed in respectable streets, those horrible motors. I seen it before, skulking round here. Horrid black thing, like a big beetle.'

'She's alive,' I said. 'But we need to get her a doctor.'

The two men arrived, puffing. 'Are you all right?' asked the workman. 'That bleeding motor – pardon my French – went straight for you. Like he wanted to hit you.'

The policeman dropped to his knees beside Mrs Jameson and checked her pulse. 'Go and find a taxi,' he told the workman. 'Quick as you can. We'll take her to the University College Hospital; it's not far.'

The workman raced off.

'Bring out some blankets,' the constable told the housemaid. She too scuttled off. 'Can you hear me, Madam? This is Constable Wandle,' he bellowed at Mrs Jameson.

She opened her eyes for a second. 'Don't call me Madam,'

she said, faintly. Then she closed them again.

Thank goodness, I thought. She was going to be all right.

'I think her ankle's broken,' I said. 'Her name is Mrs Jameson. I'm her secretary. The car…' I closed my eyes for a second. It seemed almost impossible. 'It drove straight at us. It meant to hit us; I'm sure it did.'

Constable Wandle wrote down what I told him. The maid arrived back with a blanket, which she helped me tuck around Mrs Jameson. I realised I was shivering too. Shock, I supposed.

I looked up. Mr and Mrs Clegg were standing at the doorway of their house, watching. Mr Clegg had his arm around his wife's shoulders, and they were both smiling. Had they arranged this? I wondered. Another 'accident', a swift end to this new threat to their happiness? I vowed I would find out about Lydia Clegg and her secrets.

The taxicab arrived and the men lifted Mrs Jameson in as carefully as they could, although she moaned horribly.

'You'd better go inside with her,' Constable Wandle told me. 'I'll sit up front. I know the doctors at the hospital. We'll get your lady looked after, don't you worry, Miss.'

I nodded and climbed in. Then I had a thought.

'Constable – you'd better let Inspector Peter Chadwick know about this. She's a friend of his, and we are investigating the same case.'

Chapter 21

Poor Mrs Jameson had an egg-shaped lump on her temple and her hair was matted with blood. By the time we arrived at the hospital, she had fully regained consciousness, but was paper-white and woozy with pain.

'She has a concussion from hitting her head on the ground,' the doctor told me, once he realised that I understood what he was talking about. 'We will need to keep her under observation. The left tibula is broken, too. She must keep all weight off her foot for at least six weeks. The shoulder took the main force of the collision. It has dislocated, but I can put that back in easily. The minor bruises and scrapes should heal quickly.'

Mrs Jameson was sitting up in bed in a side room, while a pair of nurses cleaned and dressed the wounds. She'd already instructed them in how to address her and had begun firing questions and instructions at me. I could see she was going to be a most impatient patient.

'Have you called Peter?' she asked. 'I don't believe for a moment that this was an accident.'

I heard a commotion outside and a furious Inspector Chadwick shouldered his way into the room, a protesting nurse close behind him.

'This is outrageous,' he shouted. 'I should never have let you get involved.'

He stomped around the little side-room, berating himself and making dreadful threats about what he would do to the driver of the motorcar when he found him.

'And we will find the devil. And he'll be on an attempted murder charge, not careless driving,' he warned.

The room was too small for this level of drama. The doctor was looking more and more irritated.

'I'm going to have to ask you to leave, Inspector,' he said, eventually. 'You're getting in the way of the nurses.'

'But I'm investigating a murder – and an attempted murder, too! You can't throw me out.'

The doctor gave him a level look. 'I am treating my patient, in my hospital. And I am throwing you out, right now.'

'I'll speak to you later, Peter,' said Mrs Jameson. Moodily, Inspector Chadwick slouched out of the door.

I sat in a chair in the corner. Now that the immediate danger was over, I was feeling shaky, almost tearful. I knew it was just a reaction to the shock, but I really needed a cup of tea. I could hear the inspector stomping around outside, no doubt annoying the porters and nurses.

I stepped out into the corridor. 'The doctor will be at least another hour,' I told him. 'Why don't we go and get some tea? There's a stall just outside on Gower Street.'

We walked down the steps from the gothic red-brick building of University College Hospital.

'I'm being a nuisance, aren't I?' said the inspector, gloomily. 'I should get back to work. We're searching the house in Sidmouth Street. All we've discovered so far is that Elizabeth Norris might have liked making money, but she didn't like to spend it. We've found jars full of sovereigns and half-crowns;

envelopes stuffed with five pound notes hidden all over the place.'

'You haven't found the murder weapon?' I asked. I wondered if Constable Yates was still searching through the bushes of St George's Gardens.

'We have, actually. It's the sort of knife that artists use to cut canvas to size. A very sharp blade mounted in a cleft handle. Perfect for the job. It had been wrapped in last week's *Daily Mail* and dumped in a litter bin on the far side of the park.'

An artist's knife. Which meant it could have belonged to Ralph Garrett, or even Hugh, I thought. That wasn't going to help.

The inspector bought two cups of tea and slices of fruitcake from the street stall, and we sat on the stone steps in the hospital's small vestibule to take our refreshments. The noise of motor vehicles on the Euston Road roared in the background. Across the street, I could see the Roman-style dome and portico of the University College London. The Slade School, I remembered, was housed in the university. The school where Ralph studied, and Hugh taught.

'Is Hugh still under arrest?' I asked. I'd hoped that our alibi for Hugh would have got him out of trouble. 'What about all the other people Mrs Norris was blackmailing? Aren't you going to talk to them?'

'Listen, Miss Swallow, I want you to tell Iris to drop all this. I shouldn't have let her get involved, but she's so damned – apologies – she's so very good at it. But it's dangerous. She's stirred up a real wasps' nest.'

He hadn't answered my question. And I was pretty certain nothing I could say would persuade Mrs Jameson to drop the case.

'We met two of the wasps this afternoon,' I said. 'I think you should interview them, at least. They stood in their doorway and watched, while we waited for the ambulance. And their maid said she'd seen that car in the square before. I wouldn't be surprised if they organised it. Another convenient accident.'

'Tell me more.'

I explained about our visit to the Cleggs, and our conviction that Mr Clegg's former wife had not met an accidental death.

'Hmm. I remember the Clegg case. We all thought it very suspicious, but the coroner ruled accidental death and the commissioner said we should drop it. If they were being blackmailed by Betty Norris, they certainly have a motive,' he said. 'But if you didn't tell them you were coming, they would not have had time to organise the car accident, would they?'

I supposed not. 'Unless they telephoned their henchman when we first arrived,' I said.

Inspector Chadwick's moustache twitched. 'Henchman, eh? Well, we should certainly check their alibi for last night. Where did they say they were?'

'The New Criterion on Piccadilly Circus, the Italian Roof Gardens.' Not far from the Café Royal on Regent Street, where Hugh had said he was going. All our suspects seemed to have converged on Piccadilly.

He made a note in his pocketbook. 'I'll send someone along to talk to the staff.'

I may have made a disappointed squeak. He looked at me, surprised.

'You're not to go by yourself, Miss Swallow. It's one thing for Iris to put herself in danger. She is at least trained to look after herself. I won't have an innocent young girl mixing herself up in such things.'

I could have pointed out that the innocent girl had saved the trained woman's life that afternoon, but I wasn't going to argue about it now. I swallowed the last of my cake and tea, then was overcome by an enormous yawn. We hadn't stopped since the telephone rang that morning, and I wasn't used to late nights. I felt as tired as I'd ever done during the drudgery of a long shift at the hospital.

'What time is it?'

'Almost six o'clock. Why don't you go home, Miss Swallow? My men have the case well in hand, I can assure you.' I looked up, suspicious that he was laughing at me again.

Mrs Jameson had asked me to bring her nightclothes and toiletries from the hotel, along with her correspondence and the evening newspapers.

'Just tell me if Hugh is free. Put my mind at rest, then I'll go back to the hotel and collect Mrs Jameson's things. And then I'll go home.' I yawned again, not bothering to cover my mouth this time.

'All right. He's being freed this evening. You look exhausted, Miss Swallow. Let's get you a taxi.'

Chapter 22

I was up bright and early on Saturday morning. A night at home in my own bed, with the sound of my father's gentle snoring coming through the wall, had sorted me out. I boarded the tram well set up for the day, with Mum's porridge sitting solidly in my stomach.

I went through my notes as the tram rattled into the Kingsway tunnel. With Mrs Jameson laid up in hospital, the best thing I could do was carry on with our plan of talking to the blackmail suspects.

Two names remained on the list: Herbert Bellamy, vicar of St George the Martyr in Queen Square, and Olive Dupont, 'therapeutic masseuse' of Argyle Street in Kings Cross. I was a bit scared of the latter and decided to tackle the vicar first.

I got off the tram at Holborn and trooped up the stairs with the yawning shop girls and clerks in bowler hats. The wide sweep of Kingsway was busy with tradesmen's vans, taxicabs, and omnibuses. It had rained overnight, but the sun was out, flashing from puddles and glittering on the raindrops that still clung to office windows.

I plunged into the flow of pedestrians, then turned north into a quieter side street with only a strip of pale blue sky visible between the tall rows of dwellings. I was soon standing at one end of leafy Queen Square, the white-painted church of St George the Martyr ahead of me.

I stepped into a big rectangular nave with slim white pillars and a lovely ceiling in white and gold. A woman wrapped in a flowery overall was sorting through a pile of hymn books at the back of the church. I approached with my brightest smile.

'Hello, dear. Have you come about the missionary fund?' she asked. 'Only the vicar's gone out. He'll probably be about an hour. Do you want to wait and have a cuppa?'

'Oh, that's a pity,' I said. 'I hoped to catch him early. I have such a busy day ahead, what with all the new missionaries to equip and send off to Africa on Monday.' My conscience pricked at telling such a blatant lie in church. I hoped God would understand the situation.

She stacked the books back onto a trolley. 'Well, I suppose you might catch him. He's only just left. But don't tell him I told you.' She came out into the square with me and shaded her eyes. 'That's him, dear. At the far end of the gardens, going into Queen Anne's Walk.'

I got a glimpse of a short, hunched figure in clerical black with a wide-brimmed hat. He disappeared into a narrow alleyway.

'Thank you so much,' I said. I ran down the square, skirting around a parade of nurses in starched aprons pushing invalid carriages from the children's hospital in Great Ormond Street. Bursting out of the alleyway, I looked left towards Russell Square, then right. There he was, heading down the road towards the Foundling Hospital. Perhaps he had business with the charity there.

I put on a spurt, thankful that I had on my old flat-heeled lace-up Oxfords and not my new satin T-bar evening shoes. As

I closed the gap, he turned left and then cut across yet another garden square with big, drooping trees. He was almost at the doors of the orphanage.

I expected him to go in, but he paused. Something about his furtive air made me dodge behind a tree while I caught my breath. He looked all around, then slipped through another alleyway.

Following discreetly, I realised with a shock that it led into St George's Gardens. The little figure ahead of me bustled through the park, now empty of searching policemen, and out via the alleyway beside the Norris residence on Sidmouth Street.

It's said that murderers are drawn to return to the scene of the crime. Was that what the vicar was doing? I pulled down my hat and kept to the shadows, all thoughts of accosting him dropped for now. Perhaps I was finally on the trail of the real killer.

Loitering at the end of the footpath, I saw him pause and look up at the house. His hat shaded his face, but I was close enough to see that his expression was troubled. He bowed his head for a moment and his lips moved in silent prayer. He wasn't gloating or cackling like a homicidal maniac. Would he knock on the door and talk to Mrs Norris's son? Perhaps that was all this was – a kindly vicar visiting his recently bereaved parishioner. I started to feel foolish, not to mention guilty, for my suspicions.

But no. He didn't go in, but turned left, crossed over Sidmouth Street, cut through a mews and into more narrow streets. We were going north, the dwellings getting smaller and more ramshackle. Dingy boarding houses with grand names like The Caledonian and The Alhambra hinted that we were approaching the railway stations.

Reverend Bellamy turned sharply into Argyle Street. Light dawned. I slid behind a parked rag and bone cart and looked in my pocketbook. Olive Dupont, number 35.

I peeked out to see him look furtively up and down the street, then trot down the stairs to the basement. I waited to hear the door shut, then strolled past, checking the house number. Unless he was urging a sinner to repent, I might have worked out why Mrs Norris had been blackmailing the Reverend Herbert Bellamy.

It wasn't really a place to linger. The rag and bone man came back, carrying a rusty old bedstead which he flung into the cart.

'You lost, sweetheart?' he asked. 'If you're looking for business, you need to get up to the street next to the station. Indoor trade only in Argyle Street.'

'Completely lost, hopeless,' I agreed hastily. 'I'm looking for Kings Cross railway station. Off to Edinburgh. Thank you so much.'

I walked briskly to the busy Euston Road, crossed it, and ran into the Great Northern Hotel. I looked at the big clock over the reception desk. It was still only half past nine.

'Can I help you, Miss?'

I allowed the boy to show me into the restaurant, where I drank a cup of very bad coffee and tried to make calculations for which I lacked much of the necessary information. The woman in the church said the Reverend would be out for an hour, and we'd taken twenty minutes to get here. Twenty minutes to get back. Twenty minutes to… conduct his business?

I had very little idea about what Olive Dupont and Herbert

Bellamy might be doing, or how long it might take. Nor, to be truthful, did I really want to know. I had gleaned certain information, of course, in the hospital. But Heidi had said Olive Dupont provided specialised services, and to those I firmly closed my mind.

I wondered what Mrs Jameson would say when I told her. She wouldn't be shocked. She never seemed shocked. She'd probably find it funny. I thought again about the question mark that Betty Norris had pencilled next to Mrs Jameson's name. What had she hoped to use against her? I remembered our conversation, how she'd pressed me about Mrs Jameson's situation and her late husband. Husband, the word she'd scribbled next to the question mark.

I pushed away the bitter dregs of coffee and left enough coins to cover my bill. It was almost ten to ten.

Chapter 23

Taking a deep breath for courage, I knocked on the basement door.

'You're early! Hold your horses, dearie.' The woman's voice was low, pleasant, and reminded me a bit of Mrs Jameson, without the American accent.

The door opened.

'Blimey O'Reilly.' A woman with bright ginger hair piled up on her head and equally startling red lipstick stared at me. She was full-figured, wore a black silk negligee and held a leather riding crop in one hand. 'Sorry, dearie, if you're selling something I don't want it, and if you want to save me, I'm past salvation.' She moved to shut the door.

'I'm here about Betty Norris,' I said, sticking my foot in the way and feeling thankful again for stout shoes.

'Oh, Lord. Come in, then. I knew it was too good to be true. She is really dead, isn't she?'

'She is.'

'And thank the Lord for that.' She looked me up and down in the hallway. 'Did he send you, then? You don't look like one of his usual types. You want to watch yourself, dearie, getting mixed up with him. Gets a bit nasty when he's had a few, if you know what I mean.'

102

I was completely out of my depth. Who did she think had sent me?

'I'm not here for anyone else,' I said. 'I'm investigating Mrs Norris's death. I'm talking to all her known associates.' I'd been impressed with Mrs Jameson's legal phrases when she was talking to the Cleggs.

Olive Dupont sat on the stairs and laughed, a hearty, full-throated chuckle. 'You? Pull the other one, it's got knobs on. Get away with you. I've got a client due in five minutes and I need to get changed.' She unrolled her scarlet stockings, unleashing a powerful smell of cheesy feet as she pulled them off.

'I saw the vicar come down here,' I said. 'Half an hour ago.'

She shrugged. 'Did you, dearie? We're organising a prayer meeting for the fallen women of Bloomsbury. Want to come along?'

'I know Mrs Norris was blackmailing him. I suppose it was because he came here. And she was blackmailing you, too. Wasn't she?'

She sighed. 'Not exactly. Listen, I'm in a hurry. If I tell you, will you go away and leave a girl in peace?'

I nodded.

'Betty was a blackmailer, all right. She had her teeth into half of Bloomsbury, including poor Herbert, who never hurt a fly. He's gone, by the way. Just managed a quick pastoral visit. In and out, that's Bert.'

She grinned, showing a row of surprisingly good teeth for her age.

'I don't care if people know how I make a living. All good advertising, if you ask me. But she could make it difficult; get the neighbours to complain and so on. She organised a police raid with her friends in the local constabulary. That was enough. But I told her: we're both businesswomen. Neither of us likes parting with cash if we can help it. We came to an arrangement.'

I waited, using the lengthy pause technique. It worked.

She sighed again. 'I paid a modest monthly amount. And I gave her a few names, just a couple a year, if they had money. In exchange, she stayed off my back. All right? Only the ones who had plenty of the wherewithal. Don't look so shocked. A girl's got to live. And I wasn't the only one feeding the rich to Betty Norris, I can tell you.'

'You told her about the vicar?' I asked. 'That doesn't seem very fair.'

She looked indignant. 'Of course not. Poor old Bert can barely find the wherewithal for our regular morning prayers. She already knew about him. In fact, I think that's how she got onto me. He had to drop a few names too, just to keep her happy.'

This was even worse. If you couldn't trust a vicar to keep a secret, who could you trust? I remembered the point of my visit was to investigate Mrs Norris's murder, not judge the ethics of the suspects.

'One last question, then I'll go. Where were you on Thursday night, between the hours of midnight and two?' I asked.

She smirked and picked up an appointment book next to the telephone. 'Let me see. I had some special guests for the evening. They stayed late. One's a member of parliament, one is a businessman whose company name you would recognise, and one is a senior police officer. So, there's no chance at all that they would provide an alibi if it came to court.

'Now, if you don't mind? Or do you want to audition as my

new dungeon-mistress? I'll have to hang up my handcuffs one day soon. Pretty girl like you could be very popular, especially with that poshed-up voice. The clients like a bit of class.'

Chapter 24

I arrived at the hospital at the same time as Inspector Chadwick. He alighted from his motor car just as my omnibus pulled up on the Euston Road.

'Visiting the invalid?' he asked.

'I am now.' I wondered what he'd say if he knew I'd just been interviewing a dungeon mistress about her clientele.

'So am I.' He was holding a bunch of bronze chrysanthemums rather awkwardly. I wondered again how well he and Mrs Jameson knew each other. Surely the relationship wasn't romantic. The inspector was in his early forties, perhaps ten years younger than her. Maybe they were just old friends, like she said.

Mrs Jameson was sitting in a wheeled chair with her leg raised. It was encased in a cast from knee to toe. The bruise on her temple was a vivid purple, matching her dress coat and turban.

'Please don't tell me what a fright I look – I can tell by your faces. I feel fighting fit, if only it wasn't for this wretched ankle. Oh, those are pretty, Peter. Thank you. Marjorie, can you put them in water? Now, what's been happening?'

I busied myself finding a vase and arranging the heavy blooms, while the inspector brought Mrs Jameson up to date about the discovery of the murder weapon – 'No fingerprints, of course, they're all wise to that these days,' – the release of Hugh Williams and the case against Ralph Garrett.

'I shouldn't tell you, seeing as his family are your clients. But it doesn't look good. He admits to having owned the drawing that was found in Mrs Norris's pocket. Coutts Bank won't talk to us, but his sister told us that money has been disappearing in large cash withdrawals from their account. Garrett has admitted giving Mrs Norris money, but won't tell us why. And worst of all, he won't tell us what he was up to on Thursday night.'

She tapped her fingers on her chin. 'There's something odd about that sketch. Why was it in her pocket? And the money, too.'

Inspector Chadwick looked puzzled. 'Where else would it be, if he'd just given it to her?'

Mrs Jameson smiled. 'How like a man. Marjorie, where would Mrs Norris put a ten shilling note and a message?'

'In her handbag, I expect,' I said, filling the vase with water from the small basin in the corner.

'Exactly. But where was her handbag? She fell on top of it. Now, Peter, what would you do if you wanted to plant a great big smelly red herring for the police to chase happily after? Would you turn the body over and dig out the handbag, covering yourself in blood and disturbing the nice clear picture of what happened?'

'No,' said the inspector, slowly. 'No, I'd shove it in her coat pocket and get out, fast.'

'Quite. Had it occurred to you that the sketch might be a plant?'

He frowned. 'You mean someone is trying to frame Ralph

107

Garrett? I'll think about it. But why doesn't the lad just give us his alibi, if he has one?'

'Maybe he really was just walking around,' said Mrs Jameson. 'People do, you know.'

'I've got the commissioner constantly on the telephone. Lord Bessborough is threatening all sorts of dire consequences if we don't release Ralph. His Lordship thinks it's Hugh Williams. Says he doesn't trust the chap; something about him being Welsh. But we've been to see the girl that Williams said he was with at the Café Royal, and she confirmed his alibi. Maybe I should check with the doorman, too.'

'Probably best, dear, but you know your business,' said Mrs Jameson. 'Now, how are you getting on with the Cleggs, and the attempt on our lives? If it hadn't been for Marjorie, I'd have been squashed flat.'

I was glad she realised. I thought she might have thanked me for saving her life, but she seemed to have taken it for granted as one of my secretarial services.

Inspector Chadwick outlined the ongoing unsuccessful hunt for the car that ran into us in Fitzroy Square.

'I have a team of constables knocking on doors of all the motor garages in this part of London. I don't think he would have risked driving far. He must have known there was a chance he'd be followed. We'll find the devil,' he said.

'And what about Betty Norris's dossier?' asked Mrs Jameson. 'There must be one. Have you found it yet?'

'We've searched the house. We haven't found anything resembling a dossier,' he admitted. 'I'm talking to Mr and Mrs Clegg this morning. They've requested a lawyer, so I'll do it at Scotland Yard. They seem to have confidence in their alibi, though. And then I suppose we should check the other names on that blackmail list.'

'No need,' I said, looking up from the flowers with a satisfied smile. 'I've done them both this morning.'

My announcement had the desired electrical effect.

'The vicar and the…?' asked Inspector Chadwick, looking shocked.

'Oh, well done, Marjorie. How did it go?' asked Mrs Jameson.

I explained how I'd followed the Reverend Bellamy to Argyle Street and seen him go into Olive Dupont's basement.

'I missed him coming out again, but I had a chat with her,' I said. 'She has an alibi for Thursday night. Well, three of them, although she's worried that they might not be keen on talking to the police. Which is odd, as one of them is a policeman himself.'

Inspector Chadwick's moustache twitched. 'I see. Well done, young lady. Although we don't have an alibi for the vicar, of course.'

'No, but Olive said he wouldn't hurt a fly.' I frowned. 'Except… she said that he might have given Mrs Norris names. And that she did herself, a couple of times a year. That it was a business arrangement.'

'Interesting,' said Mrs Jameson. 'So, when she couldn't get more cash out of her victims, she used them to find other victims with better incomes. That puts a different complexion on the case. I really do think we need that dossier, don't you, Peter? Why don't you take Marjorie around to the house for a proper look?'

He was looking at me with new respect. 'All right. And I'll tell you what, Miss Swallow. We need to confirm the Cleggs' alibi at the New Criterion. It seems suspiciously public.

Perhaps you would accompany me there this evening? I've always found it helpful to have a female perspective, as you've both reminded me this morning.'

Chapter 25

To my relief, the house in Sidmouth Street was empty. I didn't like the idea of running into Mrs Norris's son again. The conversation with Olive Dupont played over in my memory. 'Did he send you?' Who had she meant? Did Royston Norris mean to carry on the blackmail business, now his mother had died? If so, I supposed he would need the dossier with all her proofs. The question was, did he have it on him, or was it still in the house?

We went up the narrow stairs from the hallway. The runner, a drab brown coconut matting, was worn and needed a good brush. The bannisters were dusty, with smeared fingerprints on the dark, varnished wood. It was not a comfortable house. It wasn't just the cramped proportions. I'd been in plenty of smaller houses that felt more homely. I couldn't fathom why Mrs Norris wouldn't spend some of her ill-gotten gains on making the place more cheerful.

Inspector Chadwick opened the door to her bedroom. 'See what you can find here, Miss Swallow. We've been through it, but you might spot something we missed.'

The room was dim and smelled unwholesome, with top notes of lilac. I thought immediately of Mrs Norris's confiding look, her hand on my arm, and shuddered.

I walked to the window and flung the pink chintz curtains wide open. The sash window was jammed shut, but I pushed until it opened. Even the coal smoke and dust of the street was preferable to the smell of that room.

The bed was rumpled. The police had obviously pulled off all the bedclothes and flung them back anyhow. I removed them, shook them out and folded them up: the faded satin eiderdown, which had once had a pretty green and pink sprig design; the heavy cream-coloured blanket; the thin cotton sheets and pillowcases. These last bore grease-patches where her head and body had rested.

I wrinkled my nose. Why wouldn't you get your linen cleaned if you could afford it? My mother wouldn't leave bed linen unchanged for more than a week and aired every room out at least daily. There was no need to live in squalor.

I lifted the mattress, ran my hands over the headboard, took the rag rug from the floor and shook it out the window, sending clouds of dust and hair billowing into the sunshine. I checked for loose floorboards, but found none.

The furniture was heavy Victorian mahogany, the sort that nobody wanted now, if they could afford to replace it with newer, lighter things. The drawers in the chest were stuffed with underclothes, cotton stockings, flannel nightclothes and heavy rubberised corsets. I picked through them gingerly, then turned to the wardrobe.

Her day dresses, blouses, skirts, and jackets hung neatly on the rails. They were a type I recognised immediately – fashionable, but skimped, with second-rate fabrics that wouldn't last. None were older than the last season; she obviously liked to look up-to-date. I felt I was beginning to understand her better. She wanted to put on a good show

112

in society, but was too careful with money to invest in quality. And her home was simply a shelter, not somewhere to take pleasure in or make nice. I wondered what sort of home she'd lived in as a child. Not a happy one, would be my guess.

'Found anything useful?' asked Inspector Chadwick, lounging against the door jamb.

'Not really,' I admitted. I turned to the dressing table with its hair-choked brush and comb. The table had a glass top with an embroidered runner beneath. The runner was quite pretty: a Japanese-style pattern of twigs and cherry blossom. It bore initials on the bottom corner: AS. Someone Mrs Norris had known? A friend, sister, mother?

'What do you know about her?' I asked Inspector Chadwick. 'She doesn't seem to have had a very happy life.'

He looked surprised. 'She did all right, I think. She'd been widowed for twenty-five years, lived here with her son since her husband died. Her husband was vicar of St George the Martyr before the Reverend Bellamy. He left her some money, and she invested in property. She didn't need money from blackmail, you know. She was making three hundred pounds a month from her rents.'

I gasped. 'She was rich! Why did she live like this, then?'

He shrugged. 'Maybe she liked it.'

I checked through the round cardboard hat-boxes stacked on top of the wardrobe. As with her clothes, the hats were poor quality, but up-to-date. One box, however, was considerably nicer than the flimsy head-bands it contained. It was lined in puffy white satin, with the name of a respectable milliner imprinted in gold. We had stocked that company's products for a while, but they had proved too expensive for our Catford clients. The style of box had changed, though. The company had added a smart blue band around the lip of the lid. This was one of the old boxes, which meant Mrs Norris had kept it since before the War.

I took out all the dyed feathers and scraps of cheap lace and ran my fingers around the lining. Yes! There was a pouch in the satin, carefully done so you would hardly know it was there.

I reached inside, drew out the contents and laid them on the lid of the hat-box.

It was a small, sad collection of treasures. A cheap necklace with a heart-shaped pendant, the metal tarnished and soft. A cambric handkerchief, with a bright blue cornflower and the letters AS embroidered neatly in the corner. And a small square photograph, faded and worn, as if it had been much handled. In it, a thin woman with a rather defeated smile sat next to an unsmiling man with the harsh demeanour of a bully. I turned it over.

'Asa Somers,' I read in faint handwriting. 'Died 1881.' AS. Mrs Norris's mother? If so, she'd have been aged between ten and twenty when her mother died. A tough time for a girl to be left motherless, although plenty were deprived of their mothers younger than that.

'What have you found?' asked Inspector Chadwick. 'Anything useful?'

I showed him. He turned the things over dismissively. 'Not really, then. That's a shame. Well done for finding them, though. Our men clearly weren't as thorough as they thought. And it might be useful to trace Mrs Norris's family.'

'Searching for things is a woman's job,' I told him, thinking of how my father could never find his spectacles, his pipe, or his slippers. Mum would stand at the door, her bright eyes darting into every corner, then walk straight to the missing object.

'Hum. You may be right.'

There was a commotion downstairs. I flinched, hearing the rough tones of Royston Norris shouting at the constable by the door. A minute later, he was looming in the doorway, his small eyes boring into me as I hurriedly re-packed his mother's treasures.

'It's disgraceful,' he shouted. 'Going through all her things. You should be ashamed of yourself.'

And I found I was, rather. It seemed sordid and sad, searching through a dead woman's possessions to find something incriminating.

'Now then,' said the inspector. 'You want us to find the person who killed her, don't you? We must do our work. We're looking for a file of papers. Information about people. I don't suppose you know where it is?'

The man folded his arms and looked straight at the inspector. Annoyingly, he didn't do that thing people do in detective novels: look guiltily to where the secret is hidden.

'I told you. You can't bring her back, so I don't care what you do. I'll look after my own affairs. I want you out of my house. D'you hear me?'

'Perhaps we should go,' I said.

He switched his gaze to me. 'Perhaps you shouldn't be here in the first place, Missy. Perhaps you should mind your own business – you, and that Yankee woman. Poking around in a dead woman's bedroom.'

I cast my eyes down, embarrassed. And then I spotted it – the section of skirting board behind the door. What can't you see? I couldn't see dust. The rest of the skirting had a film of coal-dust, but this had been wiped clean.

I tugged the inspector's sleeve. 'I want to go home,' I said. 'Can we go now?' I tried to make my voice sound young and frightened.

He looked surprised. 'Of course, if you're sure. Don't let Mr Norris put you off, though.'

'I want to go now,' I repeated.

I waited until the door closed behind us.

'Can you get him out of there?' I asked Inspector Chadwick. 'I think I know where it is.'

I slipped through the alleyway to St George's Gardens and stood in the shadow of the wall behind the house. The pile of dog-ends that I'd noticed the previous day had gone. Had the murderer stood where I was now, waiting for Mrs Norris to come hurrying across the park after her night out in Mecklenburgh Square? Perhaps he'd offered to give her money, or information.

I gazed around the green-painted benches, flowerbeds, and tombs. At the far end of the park, a small chapel of rest had been converted into a gardener's shed, incongruous under its classical pediment.

I heard shouting from the street. 'Let go of me! I've done nothing wrong. This ain't right.' Oh dear. I'd hoped it could be done without too much trouble.

'All you need to do is answer a few more questions, Royston,' said Inspector Chadwick. 'I don't want to arrest you. But if you continue to obstruct the course of justice, I will have no choice.'

I peeped from the alleyway. Norris was walking sullenly up the street, Inspector Chadwick holding firmly on to his arm. I darted to the house. The door had been left on the latch.

I tiptoed upstairs and shivered again at the smell of lilac and dirt in Betty Norris's bedroom. I dropped to my knees and pulled away the loose skirting board by the door. Rat or mouse droppings, dust – and a roll of papers, tied with string. I pulled them out. Mrs Norris's dossier. The proofs behind her blackmail.

I was sorely tempted to untie the papers then and there. But I didn't know how long I had, and I wasn't going to risk being found by Royston Norris. I bundled the roll into my handbag and slipped out of the house.

Inspector Chadwick and Norris were nowhere to be seen.

Chapter 26

I walked briskly back to the hospital.

Mrs Jameson still looked pale beneath the bruising, the lines around her eyes and mouth more pronounced. Her ankle must have pained her.

She rallied with my news and took possession of the dossier at once. 'Let me look first,' she insisted. 'I'll share anything of importance with you.'

Mrs Jameson's own name had been in Betty Norris's black book, I remembered. I suspected she wanted to discover what the woman knew about her. Despite my disappointment, I had no choice but to let her have her way.

She'd been opening her correspondence, so I sorted through the discarded telegrams and piles of letters and began to separate them. Business, social, trade, other, as I'd been taught. Checking the engagement diary, I remembered Mrs Jameson was due for dinner with the American Ambassador that evening. I'd need to telephone Grosvenor Gardens and make her excuses when I got back to The Ritz. I folded the empty envelopes and took the rubbish to the wastepaper basket. I supposed I would get to see the dossier eventually.

There was a crumpled piece of paper beside the basket, as if Mrs Jameson had scrunched it into a ball and thrown it, but missed. I glanced over my shoulder. She was absorbed in reading. I smoothed the paper on my knee.

'Them that's in glass houses shouldn't throw stones,' it read, in spiky capital letters. 'We know what happened in Rome. Stay out of what doesn't concern you, or you'll wish you had.'

I turned to glance at Mrs Jameson. She was looking straight at me, the lines between her eyes deepened into a frown.

'Throw it away,' she said. 'Pay it no attention. You'll get used to it. If you investigate affairs that people would prefer you not to, you attract these threatening letters.'

I nodded, crumpled it up again and put it in the bin.

'Was it in the letters I brought last night from The Ritz?' I asked.

She shook her head. 'No. There was no envelope. It was on my tray when my breakfast arrived this morning. I asked the nurse about it, but she claimed she hadn't seen it until I pointed it out.'

'But that's awful! Someone in the hospital must have put it there,' I said, horrified.

'Quite so. I don't intend to stay here any longer than I must. I will move back to the hotel as soon as possible.'

What had happened in Rome? I thought of Mrs Norris, pressing for information at the party. Will her husband be joining her, or is he still in Rome? I longed for a look at the dossier that Mrs Jameson was flicking through. What secrets did it hold? There were clearly many things I did not know about my employer.

She laid down the papers. 'I've been reviewing the situation,' she said, briskly. 'We have spoken to almost all the suspects, except for Hugh Williams. He was released last night, which means he may be back at work this morning.'

'Just across the road!' I exclaimed.

'Exactly. Why don't you go over to The Slade and have a chat? Remind him that his young friend Ralph is the police's primary suspect at present. See how he feels about that. Perhaps test his alibi a little.'

I popped into Mrs Jameson's private bathroom to run a comb through my hair and wash my hands and face. The fustiness of Mrs Norris's bedroom seemed to hang around me like grubby fog. I thought of Sarah's offer to show me how to add a touch of powder to my nose, or a little pink gloss to my lips. That would give me the excuse to go back and see her later today, ahead of my trip to the West End. I must ask Mrs Jameson to see what was in the dossier against Sarah before I went.

I hoped the make-up would do for me what it did for Sarah – add a touch of brightness, of glamour. If only I had time to go before my interview with Hugh. Would he like me better with a made-up face? I wondered.

I dabbed my face dry on my handkerchief and gave myself a stern look in the mirror. I was interrogating a suspect in a murder investigation, I reminded myself. It hardly mattered if he thought me attractive or not.

All the same, I re-did my hair, tucking it neatly into a low bun at the nape of my neck so it looked almost as if I'd had it shingled. I didn't want him to think I was old-fashioned, even if he was a suspect.

Chapter 27

I opened the door to the classroom as silently as I could. It had taken me some time to track down Hugh's class in the basement of the Slade School. University College London seemed remarkably free and easy compared to Evelyn's college in Cambridge. No-one had stopped me at the gate or asked me where I was going as I crossed the hemisphere of lawn in front of the classical facade.

Girls and boys wandered the corridors unchecked and unchaperoned, their heads of shining cropped hair and casual dress so similar that it was not always obvious which was which. They all had a sort of nonchalant glamour, a frankness in their gaze. Most of them were puffing away on cigarettes and seemed to be engaged in urgent discussions.

'You can't really think that one can escape the sex drive,' said a serious-faced boy to a girl who looked almost his twin. 'Dr Freud is quite clear about the sublimation of the id.' I swivelled my head to see what his companion made of this baffling statement, but she was nodding, her wide, guileless forehead creased into a frown.

Eventually I grabbed a passing adult, who pointed me down the stairs to Hugh's studio. 'They'll be finished in ten minutes,' he said. 'He won't mind if you wait at the back. Are you a new model?' He looked me up and down, as appraising as the rag and bone man in Argyle Street.

The classroom smelled of turps and chalk dust. Perhaps twenty students stood in a circle. Hugh was opposite me, standing next to a student, pointing at something on her easel. He looked up at the sound of the door, gave a quick, surprised smile and gestured to the wooden chairs stacked up at the back of the room.

I took a seat and gazed with interest at the scene. The students were all using black charcoal, much of which had smudged onto their hands and faces so they looked like a collection of chimney sweeps. They wore aprons or smocks, liberally splashed with the materials of their art, and their faces had the same serious focus as the students upstairs. In the centre of the circle, they had posed a skeleton on one of the hard-backed wooden chairs, its legs crossed, and a trilby hat perched rakishly on its skull.

'Look at the angle,' Hugh was saying, his voice patient. 'See where the elbow turns, and how the forearm rests.' The girl frowned, reached out and corrected something, then looked to Hugh for approval.

'Better,' he said. 'Now, how does that affect where you've placed the hand?'

I looked at the papers pinned to the easels on my side of the room. One young man had produced a detailed and quite accurate portrayal of the skeleton's hat, but nothing else. A tiny girl with curly black hair, quite swamped by what looked like workmen's overalls, reached across her paper with confident gestures, sketching an impression of the bony model which looked more alive than it did. I smiled, wondering how she had learned to do it.

Hugh circled the room, stopping to assess each student's progress and give a gentle word of encouragement or correction. They liked him, I could see; looked to him with eager faces that craved his approval. Even when he got to the man with the hat, he simply laughed.

'Very good, Watson. Now, you have two minutes to do the rest.'

The students finally rolled up their drawings and filed out. Hugh went to the big sink under the window and sluiced the charcoal from his hands, then grabbed a chair and turned it backwards, sitting astride. He grinned at me.

'I know you're keen on art, Marjorie. I didn't realise you were thinking of signing up.'

'Oh...' I felt flustered. 'I'd love to learn to draw one day. Like that girl with the black curls. I thought her drawing was awfully good. But that's not why I'm here.'

'Nan. Yes, she's got talent. And she seems to understand the point of learning anatomy, which is more than most of them do. If you understand how the bones articulate, you'll do better when you move onto a life model. It's hardly new. Da Vinci did it, but some of them think they're too modern to need it.'

I smiled. 'They do seem very modern. I feel quite old-fashioned here, and I'm only twenty-four.'

His eyes rested on me, and I felt myself appraised by a man for the third time that day. Somehow, I minded it less from Hugh.

'You have an old-fashioned face,' he said. 'And all the nicer for it. I think there's a difference, you know, with the War. These students were children when we were doing our bit. They're not weighed down with it. They think it was all

123

too stupid for words, and that Bolshevism or the League of Nations or psychoanalysis will make war obsolete. That's one of the reasons I enjoy them. All that optimism is refreshing. Now, if you haven't come to learn painting, how can I help you? I suppose it's about poor Betty.'

Of all the people I'd spoken to, I realised, he was the first to express any sympathy towards the murdered woman.

'That's right,' I said. 'Mrs Jameson has been engaged by Lord Bessborough to investigate the murder. Ralph's brother, you know. Ralph is still in custody. Inspector Chadwick says it doesn't look good for him. He doesn't have an alibi, you see. And we think he was being blackmailed by Mrs Norris.'

Hugh rolled a cigarette as I spoke, then lit it and blew out the smoke before speaking. He watched it curl towards the ceiling.

'I'm sure he was,' he said. 'Many people were, as I expect you have discovered.'

'Were you?' I asked. It seemed wise to be straight about these things. Better than pretending, like I had with Sarah.

'Not exactly,' he said. 'I mean, I haven't any money. You can't get blood from a stone, no matter how hard you squeeze.'

'Why?'

'Why was she trying to blackmail a penniless artist?' Hugh's lips twisted into a wry smile. 'Well, what do you think? What are the usual reasons?'

I thought of what we had discovered. 'Bigamy. A covered-up murder. One I don't know. And – well – sex.' I tried to sound frank and open, like the students at the Slade and Evelyn's friends at Cambridge.

'You've found a covered-up murder? Miss Swallow, I salute you.' Hugh laughed. 'It's usually tawdrier than that, though, isn't it? As you've discovered. Sex.'

The word hung in the air between us. I knew my cheeks had gone crimson. I couldn't bring myself to ask another direct question.

'But in your case...' I began.

'In my case, too. I'm sure you are far too well-brought-up to ask me to supply the details.'

I was. 'That's quite sufficient, thank you,' I said, hating the primness in my voice. All the same, I wished I didn't know. I remembered what Olive Dupont had told me. She had supplied names. And she'd said she wasn't the only one who 'fed the rich' to Mrs Norris.

Eileen Power had said Hugh had asked to bring Mrs Norris to the party as his guest, to meet new people. And Winifred Garrett said she'd first met Mrs Norris at an art exhibition organised by Hugh at The Slade. From my inspection of her house, Mrs Norris didn't seem to be much of an art lover.

'Hugh?'

'Marjorie.'

'Do you know why Mrs Norris was blackmailing Ralph?'

He stretched out his legs, took another drag from his cigarette and stared at the ceiling again.

'Yes.'

'And was it...?'

'Sex? Yes, of course. He's an eighteen-year-old boy. What else would it be?'

'And...' I swallowed, 'did you tell Mrs Norris about Ralph's secret? To keep her quiet about yours?'

He exhaled, a long sigh. When he turned to look at me again, there was defiance and shame in his brown eyes.

'I didn't tip her off. That was someone closer to home, I

125

think. But I might have supplied a few corroborating details. Ralph's got plenty of money.'

I sighed. I'd really hoped I was wrong about Hugh. To be the victim of blackmail, to have made a mistake and been caught in a blackmailer's net, was one thing. But to betray a friend, a student – that was pretty unforgiveable.

'You told Mrs Norris his secrets?'

'I know. It's frightful, isn't it? But that's the thing, Marjorie. I have to live, like it or not. I need this job. I can't fall back on my family, like Ralph can. Like you can, I expect. We all do what we must, including Betty Norris.'

'She had plenty of money too,' I retorted. 'Bundles of it, all over the house.'

He smiled. 'I know. Poor old dear. It was the one thing that made her feel safe. And even that wasn't enough, in the end.'

He took a deep breath. 'Look, I've been properly poor, like she was as a kid. The sort of poverty that makes people turn their faces away in disgust. Empty belly, nowhere to sleep, barefoot poor. You'd do anything not to be back there. The money was her insurance against it. She told me about it, once. It'd make the hairs on your neck stand up.' His voice was uncharacteristically fierce.

'Her mother was beaten to death by her rotten, drunken father when Betty was twelve. She saw it happen. She ran away from home, all the way from Grimsby to London. I won't tell you how she survived on the streets, but you can guess. Eventually she got picked up by some charity and went into domestic service. She became housekeeper to a widowed vicar, and he married her, much to the horror of his family. She had a child, a husband with a bit of money, which she turned into more, using her own talents, after he died. Finally, she got rich. And she was never going back.'

I thought about the photograph of Betty's murdered mother, Asa. She'd kept her mother's embroidered handkerchief and the cheap pendant. She'd preserved them, through all that had happened to her.

'And someone killed her for it,' I said. 'Not the money. They left that. But because she was blackmailing.'

He sighed. 'That's the pity of it. I don't suppose you've worked out who it was yet, have you? I mean, I know it wasn't Ralph. I'm sure his brother will manage to get him off, sooner or later. People like that don't hang for murder.'

'Well, you're still a suspect,' I told him, not wanting to let him off the hook too easily. 'Inspector Chadwick is suspicious. He says he's going to check your alibi with the staff at the Café Royal.'

Hugh overbalanced on his chair and dropped his cigarette and tobacco tin.

'Hell. No, don't worry, I'll get it.'

He set the chair upright and started to pick up the shreds of tobacco from the paint-spattered floorboards.

I got down and helped him. 'Hugh?'

He sighed. 'Marjorie.'

'Did you really go to the Café Royal?'

He sat back on his heels and looked at me, a long, measured look. 'I didn't kill her, Marjorie.'

Chapter 28

We walked up the stairs and out into the quadrangle, where the sun shone onto the steps below the dome.

'Come on. Let's sit up here,' he said. 'It's freezing in the basement when you're not moving about. At least we can sit in the sun. And I'm starved. I'll get us some buns from the student café, and a mug of tea.'

From where we were sitting, I could see across the road to the steps of University College Hospital, where I'd sat having tea and cake with Inspector Chadwick the day before. This job involved a surprising amount of outdoor dining.

'I think you're going to make an excellent detective,' Hugh said, handing me a mug of very strong, hot tea. 'I've already told you more than I told Scotland Yard's finest during the whole of yesterday.'

'Then tell me the rest,' I said. 'Where did you go? I don't think you had time to walk all the way back to Sidmouth Street and kill Mrs Norris. I think she was killed as soon as she got home, which would have been ten minutes after she left. It was later than that by the time we got to Piccadilly Circus.'

He sighed. 'I'll tell you if you promise not to tell anyone else. Including your Inspector Chadwick. I went to a night-club.'

That didn't sound too bad. 'Well, that's good, then. You can get the people at the club to give you an alibi.' I took a bite of bun, which tasted more of bicarbonate of soda than it did of cinnamon.

'Not this club. I met Ralph there, you see. We were both there till – I don't know – two, three o'clock. Then we went back to my studio.'

I almost choked, spitting out crumbs. 'Ralph was there? He's innocent – and you know it! Why haven't you told the police? Hugh, it's serious. He really could hang for this, you know.'

He swigged his tea and gazed across the street. 'He won't. His family will get him off. The police don't have anything definite against him, do they?'

I was speechless. Hugh had an alibi for Ralph, but he'd let him stew in the police station for two days, knowing he was innocent.

I found my voice again. 'Explain,' I said. I wasn't taking any nonsense now. 'Tell me where you were and what time Ralph joined you, and why you've kept this from the police. I can't help either of you unless I know.'

He gave me a sad smile. 'I trust you, Marjorie. But you must promise not to tell the police. I mean, I've lied to them already. I've asked a girl who models for me to say she met me at the Café Royal. And it would have repercussions – serious repercussions – if the police knew where Ralph had really been.'

I didn't like it. If I kept it to myself, I would be complicit in an innocent man's conviction for murder. But perhaps if I knew, I could find another way to prove his innocence without betraying Hugh's confidence.

'I won't tell the police what you tell me,' I said. 'I promise. But I don't promise not to pester you to tell them yourself.'

129

He smiled, the teasing look back in his eyes. 'I would expect nothing less of you. God, Marjorie, why didn't I have a little sister like you to keep me on the straight and narrow? I never would have left home.'

For a moment, I imagined him as a young boy, his chestnut curls tousled from running in the streets, his charming smile fresh and childlike. He took an enormous bite of cinnamon bun. I thought with a pang of James, my beloved older brother, who had never come back from the War. James, who died aged twenty-three at dawn on Armistice Day.

'Pretend I am your sister,' I said. 'Tell me all.'

He finished chewing and composed himself, his forearms on his knees, looking at the ground. I had an urge to tuck my hand into his arm as I used to with James when we shared secrets to be kept from our parents.

'You... you know about Oscar Wilde, I suppose?'

That wasn't what I had been expecting. 'I've read *The Happy Prince*. And I once saw a production of *Lady Windermere's Fan*.'

He smiled, his lip twisting. He seemed half defiant, half ashamed. 'I don't mean his literary works. His... his crime.'

'Oh. Yes, I know.' I had asked James about it once, and he'd told me. Before the War, I'd thought it was dreadful. Since the hospital, I'd realised there were many worse things that could be done to a person's body.

'Well, that's me. Not always, but some of the time. And Ralph. More so, I don't think he likes girls at all. And the club we went to on Thursday night – it's for men like us. Some women, too. Caravanserai, they call it. It's in Ham Yard, north of Piccadilly Circus on the Soho side. I went straight there after you dropped me from the taxi. Ralph arrived about fifteen minutes later, out of breath. He'd run all the way from

Doughty Street, poor boy.

'The police know the club, of course. They raid it from time to time, but we usually get plenty of warning. It's safe enough. But I don't think anyone there would stand up in court and swear to the presence of the Honourable Ralph Garrett and the dishonourable Hugh Williams, between the hours of midnight and three in the morning.'

I was almost surprised that I was not more shocked. Perhaps at some level I'd known all along. I looked sideways at Hugh, his proud, handsome face stripped of its usual easy-going charm. There was nothing to mark him out, none of the terrible signs that the newspapers warned about: hollow eyes or degenerate posture, sloping shoulders or wasted muscles. He looked what he was – a strong, healthy, attractive man. Perhaps, whispered a voice at the back of my mind, he just hadn't met the right girl yet.

I was struck by a new thought.

'Are you and Ralph – I mean, is he your…?' I didn't have the words.

'Sometimes. It's complicated,' he said. He stared across the road, his face bleak. 'I like him very much. He has talent, and he's good company when he's not in a bad mood, like he was on Thursday. And I know he likes me.'

But you're prepared to leave him in police custody when you know he's innocent, I thought. I didn't understand.

'I think it's a great pity that you won't tell the police where you were,' I said, my voice firm. 'They are looking for a murderer, not…'

'A sodomite?' supplied Hugh. 'No, but they're usually happy enough to arrest one, all the same. I'd lose my job, of course. Especially because I took Ralph there with me. And can you

131

imagine what his family would make of it? That awful brother. Poor Ralph is terrified of him. I honestly think he'd rather stay in prison than face Lord Bessborough if this came out.'

It was quite a pickle, I could see. But I had faith that someone like Inspector Chadwick, who seemed so intelligent and kind, would be able to use the information without exposing the source of it. I committed to memory the name of the club: Caravanserai. I liked it; it sounded mysterious and eastern, like something from the *Arabian Nights*.

'Have you met Lord Bessborough?' I asked. 'He came to Miss Power's house, the morning after the murder. He was so pompous, but Mrs Jameson handled him beautifully.'

Hugh laughed. 'I'll bet she did. He came to a show of Ralph's pictures at the Slade, with that man of his. Jack Hudson.'

There was an edge to his voice.

'You know his man, then?' I asked.

'He still owes me five quid. We were in Belgium together, for a while. He owed everyone money, mainly from cards. Then he got moved to Bessborough's regiment and the next thing I heard he had a nice cushy desk job at headquarters, managing supplies or something. Always comes out on top, Jack. I couldn't believe it when I saw him at the exhibition, swanning around with his Lordship.'

Mentally, I ran through the timeline, as Mrs Jameson called it. I supposed it was just about possible that Ralph had walked Winifred home after the party, gone back to Sidmouth Street and murdered Mrs Norris, then run all the way to Piccadilly. But he would have been covered in blood, and he'd not have had time to change or wash it off.

'You're sure about Ralph?' I asked. 'That he was there so quickly?'

Hugh smiled at me. 'I applaud you for taking it in such a business-like fashion, Marjorie. I worried you would faint away at the mention of it. Sex, you know.'

I gave him a severe look. 'I doubt you could find any of us that served in the VAD who'd faint at the mention of sex. We've seen worse, I can tell you. Now, Ralph.'

'All right. I'd got myself a whisky, and I was chatting with the owner. She said it had been quiet, but was livening up now that the shows were over. There was a party in from one of the big musical revues. She offered to introduce me, and I was about to go over when Ralph arrived. I hadn't even finished my drink. It couldn't have been more than about fifteen minutes.'

He grinned at me. 'He wasn't dripping with blood or carrying a knife. He spent the first ten minutes complaining about Betty getting all cosy with Winifred, and then about his brother trying to tell him he should stay at home. But I don't think he was contemplating murder.'

He turned serious for a moment. 'Ralph's more likely to do himself in, you know, than harm anyone else. I've had students like him before. It seems to be part of being an artist, for some of them. They lack the tough skin that the rest of us grow. It's like they're walking around naked, with no defences. They see beauty more than the rest of us, but they get hurt more, too. That was one of the first things I recognised about Ralph.'

Had Hugh recognised himself, from before the War? I wondered. I remembered how he told me he'd come through without a scratch, but found he could not paint anymore. He'd grown a tough skin.

'And the second thing I realised,' he said, 'was that he badly needed someone to take him to Caravanserai, before he made himself thoroughly miserable trying to be something he was not.'

Chapter 29

I returned across the road to the hospital to find Mrs Jameson ordering the nurses around and getting everything packed up to return to The Ritz.

'The food's better, and I might as well convalesce in comfort,' she said. 'Graham will look after me. I will have a telephone, and you can sleep in your little cubbyhole off the sitting room, Marjorie.'

I helped one of the nurses with the packing. She seemed suspiciously keen to get Mrs Jameson ready for departure. I suspected my employer had not been the easiest of patients. The nurse said she'd recommended a friend, Nurse Barrington, who used to work at the hospital, but now took private patients. She would meet us at The Ritz and see that Mrs Jameson had everything she needed.

'I can do that,' I protested. 'There's no need.'

'Nonsense,' said Mrs Jameson. 'I need you for the investigation, especially as I'll be confined to barracks. Now, did you find out anything interesting from Hugh? Or did you spend the afternoon gazing into his brown eyes? You've been gone a very long time.'

'I'll tell you about it later. But Ralph Garrett has an alibi, and Hugh knows it. Unfortunately, neither of them feels able to share it with the police.'

She looked at me for a minute, tapping her chin. You could almost hear the brain cells fizzing. 'I see. At least, I think I do. I take it you have abandoned romantic dreams of starving in an artist's studio with him?'

I looked away, annoyed. 'I do think you might give me some credit, Mrs Jameson. He said he'd told me more than he'd told Scotland Yard in all the time they had him in for questioning.'

She laughed her loud American laugh. 'Marjorie, you are the cat's pyjamas, as the young people say. You've worked wonders. From lying actresses to murderous wholesalers, sex-mad vicars to ladies of the night and artists with mysterious alibis. Did you think you'd find yourself in such company when you took the job of a respectable secretary?

'Now, see if you can find a taxicab that can accommodate a wheeled chair. It's time we got back to The Ritz.'

The journey was quick, but I saw the jolting pained her. The nurse was waiting upstairs in the suite, a tall, starchy-looking woman in her late twenties or early thirties with big, bony wrists sticking out of her uniform. She reminded me of the professional nurses I'd worked with at The Maudsley. Most of them were lovely, but some had resented the VADs and lost no opportunity to remind us of our lowly status. She looked like one of those.

Nurse Barrington and Graham Hargreaves settled Mrs Jameson on the sofa, her foot raised. Frank, the barman at the Rivoli Bar downstairs, sent up her favourite French 75 cocktail, which he said would have her back on her feet in no time.

'I really would not advise it,' said Nurse Barrington, firmly. Equally firmly, Mrs Jameson took the glass. She swallowed a mouthful then lay back on the pillows, her face pale and tired.

'Perhaps I need to rest,' she admitted. Nurse Barrington looked triumphant and gave me the glass to dispose of the drink.

'Nasty stuff,' she said. 'Throw it down the sink.' I resisted the temptation to finish it myself, wondering how long Mrs Jameson would put up with being told what to do. The Barrington woman began fussing around with her luggage, getting in the way of the maid who was trying to unpack.

'Marjorie, take those papers,' said Mrs Jameson. 'They should go into the safe.' I took Mrs Norris's dossier from her olive crocodile-skin reticule and transferred it to my own handbag. Could I risk a peek?

I flicked through the close-written pages with their small, cramped script. I needed to look up Sarah, after all. A page with Sarah's name at the top had fewer details than I'd hoped. A date, 29 July 1921, and a name, Kenneth Arthur Simpson. An address, Redchurch Street in Shoreditch. I scribbled it down in my pocketbook.

'We'll go through the papers later,' came Mrs Jameson's sleepy voice. 'Put them away now.'

With a sigh, I returned the dossier to my bag. I considered our suspects one by one. Ralph and Hugh had both been in the Caravanserai club until after Mrs Norris's body was discovered, although the alibi might be hard to prove. Percy Digby, bigamist and chemist, had been at home in Tottenham Court Road with one of his families, while one of his babies had colic. Olive Dupont had been entertaining clients; the Cleggs claimed to be at the Criterion, and we would check up on their alibi that evening. Inspector Chadwick had left a message to say he would call for me at seven o'clock.

That left the vicar of St George the Martyr, and Sarah. The vicar, I remembered, had taken over the parish Mrs Norris's husband had once served. Had she known the Reverend Bellamy while her clergyman husband was still alive? Perhaps she had found out about his predilections then.

I still thought both of them unlikely murderers. For one thing, Olive Dupont had indicated that Mrs Norris had been blackmailing Herbert Bellamy for many years, and the Reverend Norris had been dead for a quarter of a century. Why would Bellamy suddenly turn on her now? And Sarah, although vehement in her dislike of the woman, seemed too delicate a creature for throat-cutting.

Yet I was sure she had been lying about her return home on Thursday night. Actresses might look delicate, I reminded myself, but theirs was a demanding, physical profession. And they knew how to deceive.

It was time to find out whether Sarah was trustworthy. I checked again on Mrs Jameson, although Nurse Barrington told me there was no need, and tucked a cashmere shawl around her shoulders. I scribbled a note to tell her where I was going and headed downstairs. Handing the dossier to the receptionist to be locked away in the hotel safe, I asked them to call me yet another taxi.

Chapter 30

'Sorry to bother you again. I brought you these,' I said, glad that I had stopped to buy some violets from a street stall. Sarah looked downright hostile, with her hair wrapped up in a towel and a curious glazed look to her skin. There was a strong smell of ammonia.

'Thank you,' she said, barely moving her lips. I followed her up the stairs. The kitchen in Amwell Street was just as chaotic as it had been the day before. Two bowls sat on the table, egg yolks in one and whites in another. A brown glass bottle sat by the sink, labelled hydrogen peroxide.

Sarah put the little bunch of sweet-smelling flowers in a glass of water and washed her face at the sink.

'There, that's better. Sorry, Marjorie. I wasn't expecting anyone, so I was egging my face and touching up my roots.'

'Egging your face?' I asked, as she unwrapped the towel and poured water over her head from a jug. Peroxide bleach swirled down the drain.

She took another towel and wrapped her hair into a turban. 'You paint egg white on with a pastry brush and let it set. It's supposed to give your skin extra protein. It stops you from getting wrinkles.' She laughed. 'It's probably nonsense, but it can't hurt. And you only use a bit. I'll have the rest scrambled on toast for my tea.

'Now, what can I help you with? Have you caught that murderer yet?' She sounded a little nervous, although she hid it with laughter.

'Not yet. But I need your help for tonight. I'm going to check up on two of our main suspects, at the Italian Roof Gardens in the New Criterion. And I thought it would be the perfect time to try out wearing make-up. I want to look like I fit in,' I explained.

Her smile this time was genuine. The pinch of anxiety between her eyes had gone, smoothed over with relief.

'Of course! Gosh, lucky you. I long for the Italian Roof Gardens. I've been to the East Room for tea, with Bertie and his mother. It's ever so pretty, like a French salon, with lovely paintings and furniture. But I've not been to the Roof Gardens yet. You must report back, every detail.'

She went to her bedroom and brought out a hat box, which she set on the kitchen table. It was full of bottles, brushes, and powder puffs. She leaned a hand mirror against the toast rack.

'The light's better here than in my bedroom,' she said. 'Now, brush your hair back from your face and let me have a look at you.'

She gazed at me with a professional attitude for a few minutes, her head to one side.

'Colour, that's what you need,' she said. 'You're lucky – no spots or freckles or blemishes to hide. Your skin is fresh as a daisy. But you're pale. With that dark hair, you could take a touch more pink in your cheeks and lips. Nothing on the eyelids; it'd be too startling.'

I agreed I did not want to startle.

'I'll start with a cream to plump and smooth the skin. This

is the one I always use, because they give me a discount to recommend it to people,' she said. 'But it's good. I would use it anyway.'

She patted it over my face. It smelled strongly of rosewater.

'I'm really looking forward to it,' I confided. 'I've never been anywhere like that before. It's so exciting. A police officer is going to take me.'

'Goodness. Will he be in uniform? That will look queer,' said Sarah. 'Now, I'll massage this in.'

'No, he's a detective,' I said proudly. I had barely known the difference between one type of policeman and another a couple of weeks ago. 'He's checking all the alibis. That's why we're going to the Roof Gardens. The people in question claimed to be there, but he wants to be sure. He's going to talk to the staff. He'll be checking up on everyone, I expect. He'll probably talk to your friend – Molly, was it? And maybe your landlady, too.'

Sarah had stopped her massaging.

'Really?' She laughed, but a strained tone had come into her voice. 'I can't see why he would need to.' She reached for the block of eye-black and picked up a brush. 'Now, do you want to darken your lashes? It makes your eyes look really big.'

'I'll try it,' I said. 'I suppose they just have to be very thorough, what with it being a murder case.'

'I suppose so.' Her hand was shaking as she spat on the block and rubbed the brush into it.

'Shall I do that?' I didn't want her poking my eye out.

'Just a little, on the tips of the eyelashes,' she instructed. 'And if it rains, remember to keep your eyes open until you can dab it dry. Otherwise, it runs down your face.'

I did as she instructed and peered into the mirror. As Sarah said, the black seemed to outline my eyes and make them more definite. I quite liked it.

'Anyway,' I said. 'You had cocoa with Molly and went to bed, didn't you? There's nothing to worry about.' I'd decided it would be best to pretend I believed her.

She fiddled with the contents of the hat box. 'Do you really think he'll talk to the landlady?' she asked.

'Probably. Now, do you think that's enough?' I batted my eyelashes at her.

'I don't know.' She pulled out a big fat brush and a pot of powder. 'Marjorie?'

'What?'

She set her things down. 'Oh, I'm in such a muddle. The thing is, I did come in when I said. But only to get changed. Then I went out again.'

Here it was. I waited for her to say more.

'And I'm afraid the landlady noticed, because I saw her peeping out from behind the curtains downstairs when I got back,' she said. 'There's no sense in asking Molly to tell the police I was at home drinking cocoa from half past midnight, because that old cat downstairs knows full well I was out till gone two.'

My heart sank. 'Where did you go?'

'That's the thing. I can't tell you. I can't tell anyone. Because then it would all come out, and I'd lose all my work, and Bertie – well, I'd probably never see him again.' She flung the brush down in despair.

'Come on. It can't be that bad,' I said, filling the kettle and setting it on the stove.

'Oh, it can,' she said, darkly. 'It can be very bad indeed.' She spooned tea into the pot and rinsed a couple of cups in the sink.

Time to ask the big question. 'Mrs Norris was blackmailing you, wasn't she?'

She sighed. 'I suppose you or Mrs Jameson found out. Well, there you are, then. Yes. Yes, she was, the dreadful old thing.'

'Mrs Jameson's the detective,' I said. 'You're not the only one who was being blackmailed, if that helps at all.'

She smiled. 'Not really. Misery loves company, but I doubt that applies to blackmail victims. I know it's awful, but I can't be sorry she's dead, not really. She's the reason I can't afford anywhere decent to live, no matter how good a role I land. Now at least I'll be free of her.'

'Unless they accuse you of her murder,' I reminded her.

'Oh, goodness me, Marjorie. But they won't, will they? Do the police know she was blackmailing me?' She looked shocked.

'I think they do,' I admitted. 'There was a list.'

'But that's awful! I didn't do it. I don't even know how it happened, or anything. I mean – do you really think I could murder someone? I wouldn't know how.'

I had to smile. Her pretty face looked so childlike and innocent. But she was an actress. And she'd lied to me before.

'I'm keeping an open mind,' I said. 'At least, until I know what Mrs Norris was threatening you about, and where you went that night.'

'You mustn't tell anyone,' she said. 'I went to Shoreditch. I walked there because I didn't have the money for a taxi. It took me three quarters of an hour to get to my sister's house.'

'Your sister?' That must be the address in Redchurch Street, I supposed. 'Well, that's all right then, isn't it? Why would anyone…'

'I went to see my son,' she added. 'Kenny.'

'Oh,' I said. Kenneth Arthur Simpson, July 1921.

The kettle whistled and I poured the boiling water into the pot. Sarah brought milk from the pantry and poured two cups of rather weak tea. We sat in silence for a minute, then she explained. It was the usual story. She'd fallen in love with another actor in a play, two years previously.

'That's the thing about acting. You get so caught up in the play, and you're with the rest of the cast the whole time. It's very intense. People are always falling in love, and at the time it seems like the real thing. But the run finishes and you look at them and wonder what it was all about,' she said. 'The whole thing seems like an illusion.'

I began to understand why my father had been so against my enthusiasm for amateur dramatics at Sydenham High School.

Sarah had fallen pregnant.

'It wasn't Bertie, of course. Bertie's not like that. And if it had been, he'd have stuck by me,' she said. 'Not like that b—, pardon my language. As soon as I realised I was in trouble, he was off. What could I do?'

What she had done was find a quiet place to live where nobody knew her, recommended by one of the chorus girls. A spartan room in a house in Somerstown, north of Euston railway station, run by a woman who asked no questions and had an arrangement with a local midwife. Her name was Betty Norris.

'It was bleak, Marjorie, honestly. I've never been so lonely and scared. I told everyone I was on tour abroad for four months. And my sister – she's got two already and lost one not long after I fell – she agreed to take Kenny afterwards. Say he was her own. I go over to see him. Not too often; people would talk. But I miss him.' She wiped her nose on the back of her hand.

'So, I went round on Thursday night, to sit and watch him for a while. I do that, sometimes, just to see him sleeping. He's such a little beauty, honestly. Golden curls and round cheeks, long eyelashes. Takes after me.' She smiled fondly.

'Well, there you are. Think what you like of me, Marjorie. But now you know why I can't tell anyone. And that's what Betty Norris had on me. Soon as I left her house, she was round with her hand out: "I hadn't realised you had such a promising career," all that stuff. And the better I did, the more she threatened me. When I started walking out with Bertie, she told me she thought that he should know what sort of woman I was. And then she kept dropping hints, all through dinner on Thursday night. That's what got me so upset.'

Upset enough to want Mrs Norris dead. I could understand that. But – assuming her sister confirmed her story – she had plenty of motive, but no opportunity for the murder.

'You'll have to tell them, Sarah. Honestly, the police don't care about whether you've had a child,' I said. 'They just need to know where you were.'

'But I've lied to them already, haven't I? And Bertie – what if they ask him about it? He'll find out, and I'll lose him. I can't bear it. Why should I lose everything that's dear to me, just because...' she tailed off. 'Well, I expect you'll have your own views on that.'

Of course, I knew there were plenty who would say she'd got what was coming to her. And I'd certainly been brought up to regard my honour as something to keep well-guarded before marriage. But I'd seen young men die from wounds, clutching worn-out photographs of their girls. I quite understood why some had come through the War with the attitude that you might as well seize the day. And no doubt Sarah's profession made her vulnerable to all sorts of cads.

I thought about Bertie Post, and the way he'd looked at Sarah while they danced. He didn't strike me as a cad.

'I don't think it's anyone's business but your own,' I said, firmly. 'But I do think you should tell Bertie. I mean – won't it be awfully difficult if you get married one day? Surely, if he really loves you, he'll understand. He might even agree to have Kenny in your home. Isn't it worth trying? If you really love him, I mean.'

She squeezed my hand. 'You're sweet, Marjorie. But believe me, men don't forgive that sort of thing. Even the good ones.'

Chapter 31

Was Inspector Chadwick one of the good ones? I wondered, as he held the taxi door open for me at the Regent Street entrance of the New Criterion. Mrs Jameson certainly seemed to think so. She had agreed that Sarah was probably off the list for now. Which only left the Cleggs and the vicar. Someone had murdered Betty Norris, though. We were in danger of running out of suspects.

And if we didn't find an alternative suspect soon, Ralph Garrett could hang for a murder I knew he couldn't have committed. Or the inspector would discover that Hugh had not really been at the Café Royal and would arrest him again. I wished I could confide in Inspector Chadwick, but I had promised. I had been formulating my own plan to stand up their alibis, without betraying Hugh's confidence. I was nervous, but determined to do my bit.

We walked up the grand stairs, Inspector Chadwick half a pace ahead of me. He walked fast, his hazel eyes scanning the scene. He was broad-shouldered in his well-cut, dark tailcoat and top hat, his jaw firm, his moustache neatly trimmed. A man you felt you could depend upon. Not handsome, really, but attractive. The sort of man a girl likes to have as her escort, even if he is twenty years older.

My lilac frock and headband were enjoying their second outing. I felt slightly self-conscious about my darkened eyelashes and the pink tint on my cheeks and lips, but Sarah had assured me the cosmetics enhanced my natural charms. After her confession, she'd done my hair, curling and separating sections so they framed my face, while the length of it was held back in a loose chignon.

'You really would suit a shingle,' she'd told me. 'I'll give you the name of my hairdresser. You can't believe how freeing it is to have short hair.'

All in all, I was quite happy as we walked to the door of the Italian Roof Gardens.

It was as spectacular as I'd imagined. At each end of the long room, a tall fountain played, sparkling in the light. Around the dancefloor, white trellis grown over with real vines framed pretty pergolas, underneath which marvellously dressed people were seated for dinner. Terraces and mountains were skilfully rendered in the backdrop, and above our heads a soft midnight-blue fabric shimmered. It took me a moment to realise I was not really under a starry sky.

'Oh, how lovely!' I exclaimed.

Inspector Chadwick looked surprised, then smiled. 'It is good, isn't it? Most realistic.' He spoke to the man at the desk, and we were escorted to one of the pergolas.

'Would you like some wine, Miss Swallow? I'm officially working, so I can't join you.'

I was tempted to ask for champagne, just to see what he said. 'A glass of lemonade, please.' If I was to carry out my plan for the evening, I would need a clear head.

The Roof Garden All-Stars, a five-piece jazz band, took the stage in the middle of the dancefloor to a smattering of applause. The drummer set up a curious shuffling rhythm and three players – clarinet, trumpet, and slide trombone – stood as one and blared out the first notes of the hottest jazz I'd ever heard.

The piano took up the melody and I gasped. The player was Freddie Gillespie, who I'd last seen heading sadly back to Brixton after losing his job as pianist at The Ritz's Palm Court. I had no idea he could play like that. His hands flew over the keys, adding glissandos from the top to the bottom with panache.

'What is it?' asked Inspector Chadwick, handing me a menu.

'I know the pianist,' I said. 'He was a patient in the Maudsley Hospital when I nursed there during the War. I met him again a couple of weeks ago when he was playing at the hotel. But I didn't know he worked here.'

'Well, that might be useful. Have a word with him when they break. Find out if they were here on Thursday, and if he remembers the Cleggs' party. Now, let's order, then I'll go and have a quiet word with the restaurant manager.'

I was famished, not having eaten since my disappointing cinnamon bun with Hugh at lunchtime. I was torn between salmon en croute and chicken escalope. I wasn't sure what either of them was, but they both sounded delicious.

'Chicken, please,' I told the waiter. 'Then strawberry ice-cream. And a glass of hock.' My lemonade seemed rather too tame in this environment.

All around us, people were taking to the dancefloor, exhibiting the angular movements of the modern jazz style. I wondered how they learned. Were there dance schools to teach you to waggle your knees like that, or pump your elbows out at the sides? I remembered our games mistress at Sydenham High, grasping us against her ample bosom and parading us around the gym as she taught us a plodding waltz: 'One two three, one two three, head up, Marjorie!' I couldn't imagine her contorting her limbs like the dancers on the floor.

'What are you laughing about?' asked the inspector, back from his interrogation of the manager.

'Oh, nothing. Just watching the dancing. And remembering being taught to waltz at school,' I said.

He laughed too. 'I didn't get taught anything like that,' he said. 'Perhaps I could manage a foxtrot, at a push.'

It would be rather nice, dancing with Inspector Chadwick, I thought. The problem with most men was that they were too hesitant about leading. I suspected he would not have that problem. I remembered again dancing with Hugh, the lightness and elegance with which he moved us around the floor. Ah, well.

'What did you find out?' I pushed Hugh from my mind.

'They were booked in for the ten o'clock sitting, which fits with what they told you about eating after the theatre. But he doesn't know if they stayed all night. He's going to see if he can find their waiter.'

The food arrived and I tackled it with relish. Chicken escalope turned out to be a flattened breast of chicken, breadcrumbed and fried. I'd never had it like that before, and it was delicious. I glanced up to see the inspector smiling at me.

'You do enjoy life, don't you, Miss Swallow?'

I put down my knife and fork, hoping I hadn't been eating too fast. I thought about what he'd asked.

'I think one has to,' I said. 'After everything that's happened. So many people didn't get a chance at it, after all. The worst thing would be to let it go by, and not take notice of how good it can be.'

He nodded. 'You're right, of course. It's surprising how many people get caught up in the difficulties, and don't notice the good things.'

'Mrs Jameson enjoys the good things,' I said.

He smiled and pushed his empty plate away. 'She does. She was not always in a position to enjoy life. But she is now, and she makes the most of it.'

I decided to risk it. 'Can you tell me more about her, Mr Chadwick? Because Mrs Norris was asking me all about her former life, and there was an anonymous letter, about Rome…'

I tailed off. The smile had dropped from his face. 'When did she get an anonymous letter?' he asked.

'This morning, at the hospital. It was put onto her breakfast tray.'

'And no-one thought to tell me? Heavens, Miss Swallow. I know Iris is cavalier about her safety, but I thought better of you. What if someone had tried to harm her while she was alone in her room?'

It was hardly my place to inform the police about my employer's correspondence, but I wasn't going to point that out.

'That's why she decided to go back to The Ritz,' I said. 'But do you think it was sent by the same person who ran her over? They would guess she was in the University College Hospital, I suppose. Or they might have had someone watching and followed us there.'

His face was grim. 'What did it say?'

I tried to remember. 'We know what happened in Rome, I think. And it told her to stay out of things that didn't concern her, or she'd wish she had.' I looked up at the fake star-studded ceiling. 'That people in glass houses shouldn't throw stones.'

A waiter arrived at the table and began to stack our empty plates.

'You wanted to know about Mr Reginald Clegg's party, sir?' His voice was as smooth as the way he glided across the restaurant. 'They arrived about half an hour after the sitting began, but they stayed late. Until at least two o'clock, if memory serves. A most pleasant party, very generous. Will there be anything else?'

Reginald Clegg had said he'd given the waiter an enormous tip. Natural generosity, or to make sure he remembered him? Perhaps to ensure the man gave the story Mr Clegg wanted the police to hear. Inspector Chadwick took his name, then waved the waiter away, his brow thunderous. I supposed he thought it had all been a waste of time.

Just then, the music paused, and the band retired to take a break. Now was my chance to say hello to Freddie.

'Good Lord, is that Nurse Swallow?' He was mopping his forehead with a handkerchief after his exertions. He looked far happier than he had at The Ritz, I thought.

'Hullo, Freddie. You're a dark horse. I didn't know you played jazz,' I said.

'I play anything.' He grinned at me. 'But I like this best. I learned during the war, from a chap from New Orleans. It's exciting, don't you think? A complete break from what came before. One of the fellows in the band is from America. New York, you know, with all the latest styles. I'm learning so much.'

'That's wonderful,' I said. I looked at the glitter in his blue eyes. Had he been drinking? He seemed not just happy, but exuberant. Most unlike the Freddie I knew.

The trombone player, a tall, thin black man, winked at me, tipping up his instrument to empty it. 'You didn't tell me you had a girl, Fred. And such a cutie, too.'

I blushed, but Freddie just laughed.

'This is Nurse Marjorie Swallow. Marjorie, this is T-bone Tommy, on loan from the Harlem Swingers, the hottest trombonist in town.' He took a glass of beer from a passing waiter and downed half of it in one pull.

'I'm not a nurse anymore,' I said, smiling up at T-bone.

'I can see that, Miss,' he drawled. 'Don't look like any starched-up nurse I've ever seen.'

Freddie twisted around to see who I had been sitting with. 'You're very up-town tonight, Marjorie. Who's that with you? Your father?'

I pulled him away from the band to speak more privately. 'He's a policeman. We're here to investigate a murder,' I said. 'Were you working here on Thursday?'

He laughed so hard I had to bang him on the back. 'What, another one? Good Lord, you're serious. Right. Well. Yes, we were here on Thursday. What happened? Was someone bumped off in the powder room?'

I pulled out the photograph of the Cleggs that Inspector Chadwick had given me, cut from a newspaper report of their wedding.

'Look at this photograph. The couple in the picture. They said they were here on Thursday night, and we need to be sure if they stayed late. They were booked for the ten o'clock sitting. She's pregnant, so I don't suppose she danced much.'

He took the cutting and squinted at it. 'Hard to remember. It all blurs into one.' He called across to the trombonist. 'T-bone, was it Thursday that Edna Maud performed? She's a

153

top-notch dancer, you know, Marjorie. Does a special set a couple of times a week.'

'That's right,' said T-bone. 'She's a real live wire. Good kid, too.' He reached for the photograph in Freddie's hand. 'Yeah, I remember that baby doll. She's a real knock-out. They were in a party of four; arrived a little late, about half-past ten. They sat over here, to the left of the stage. That's out of your line of sight, Fred.'

'Splendid,' I said. 'And do you remember how long they stayed?'

He sucked his teeth. 'Right till the end, I reckon. Miss Maud did two sets that night. But this fellow,' – he pointed to Mr Clegg – 'he wasn't here the whole time. Went out at about one o'clock. I remember thinking it was a bit rotten of him, leaving his wife in her condition. But he was only gone for half an hour.'

Half an hour. A chink in the alibi, I thought gleefully. But was it enough?

'That's so clever of you,' I said. 'Thank you, Mr T-bone.'

He laughed heartily, a big deep laugh. 'You call me Tommy, like everyone else. Or T-bone. Don't need no Mistering.' He took a long swig at his glass of beer. 'Now, we gotta get going again. You ready, Freddie?'

I ran back to my seat, just in time for the strawberry ice-cream. 'They saw them,' I said, breathless. 'Mrs Clegg was here the whole time. But Mr Clegg left for half an hour, at about one o'clock.'

The inspector was instantly back in humour again. 'Well done, Miss Swallow. I wonder where he went. Now, have you finished that pudding? I'm afraid I have work to do. I'll put you in a taxi back to The Ritz.'

I swallowed the last delicious mouthful. I had work to do, too. And the scariest part of the evening lay ahead.

Chapter 32

I waited until the Inspector turned the corner of Regent Street, presumably to check up on Hugh's confected alibi at the Café Royal. I did need to establish his real one, then.

I called out to the driver. 'I say! Sorry, but can you stop? I need to get out.'

The man looked aggrieved. 'You've only just got in,' he pointed out, not without reason.

'I know. But I've forgotten something.' I passed him half a crown, which seemed to cheer him up.

I stepped out into the street and walked back along Piccadilly to the centre of the circus, where the statue of Eros perches above London with his congregation of flower-sellers, newspaper boys and loafers. A policeman stood in the middle of the junction, directing the traffic. The lights of the passing vehicles dazzled, well-dressed people glided in and out of fashionable theatres and restaurants, the illuminated advertisements shone above our heads. There was nothing to be scared about.

All the same, I pulled my old coat closer as I crossed Shaftesbury Avenue. Ham Yard, north of Piccadilly Circus, Hugh had said. With determination, I made for the narrow, barely lit Sherwood Street, a few paces but a world away from the bright lights of the circus.

Out of the glare, people lurked in the shadows. A couple of street urchins, a boy and a girl, huddled into a doorway with an old shawl wrapped around them. The girl grinned up at me, eyes bright in her dirty face.

'Penny for a bun, Miss?'

I fumbled in my purse and found one. Immediately, three or four other children emerged from behind the waste bins and held out their hands. I realised I would have half of London's feral youth surrounding me if I didn't watch out.

'Right, that's it. I've no more,' I said, having dispensed small change to half a dozen children.

'She's new,' I heard one boy say, knowledgeably.

I clutched my bag tightly under my arm. 'Can you tell me how to get to Ham Yard?' I asked him.

He put his head sideways and looked at me critically. 'Well I never. I wouldn't have taken you for one of those. All right, Miss. Turn right up that alley, just past the streetlamp. You comes out on Windmill Street. Turn right again for a bit, then look out for another alley on your left. That leads through to Ham Yard.'

I tried to keep the instructions in my head. As I passed the streetlamp, a rough-looking man detached himself from the wall and approached me. I put my head down and walked past him, ignoring his lewd suggestions. He called a foul insult after me as I hurried away, hoping he would not be tempted to follow me. I wished I had someone – ideally Inspector Chadwick, with his reassuring bulk – by my side. But anyone would have done. Hugh. Freddie. T-bone Tommy, with his big laugh.

The alleyway was completely unlit, although I could see a

glimmer of light at the end. I thought I heard footsteps behind me, but when I turned, I could see no-one. I broke into a trot.

Great Windmill Street wasn't much better when I reached it. There were street girls in the doorways, throwing me hostile looks. I'd reapplied my pink lip-tint in the powder room after my ice-cream, feeling very debonair. Now I rather wished I hadn't, although my make-up was nothing like as garish as some of the faces that turned to watch me pass, lit up by gaslight. Electricity was on its way, we were told. It couldn't come soon enough to light up these dark places.

Men strolled the street, in pairs or singly. A crowd of rowdy-looking young men in top hats and tailcoats was laughing and shouting at one end of the street, having accosted a couple of the girls. I hurried on, keeping my gaze on the ground, careful not to catch anyone's eye. Look out for an alleyway on the left, the boy had said.

I spotted one and plunged into the darkness. The place stank of rotting vegetables, urine and goodness knows what else. I thought with regret of my new T-bar satin shoes, as I stumbled over mounds of unknown rubbish. But it would have looked suspicious to bring a change of footwear. I'd been dressed for a night at the Italian Roof Gardens, whisked there and back by taxi, not for walking the alleyways of Soho.

I soon realised I was not alone in the dark alley. Rats snickered and scuttled ahead of me. Alarming noises from the shadows told me that this was where some of the girls took their clients. Sweat broke out on my forehead and my armpits pricked with it. I blushed for them, but more for myself.

There were definitely footsteps behind me now. A man's footsteps, heavy of tread. More than one man, I thought. I glanced over my shoulder, but could see nothing but shadows.

Fog had crept into the alleyway, its acrid taste bitter, stinging my eyes. I peered ahead, but could not see to the end. What had the boy said? It leads through to Ham Yard. Or was that the next one? Right, then right again. Alleyway on the left. My heart began to beat faster. I was no longer very sure of the directions.

I could hear the footsteps gaining on me. Were they really following, or was I imagining it? I should try to throw them off. I saw what looked like an opening to another street on my left and turned into it. It was unpaved, muddy and stank of horse manure. The footsteps followed. I began to run, stumbling over piles of manure and feeling the wetness creep into my poor shoes.

I almost ran into a brick wall, and gasped. A dead end? The footsteps still sounded, not hurried now, but coming my way. Definitely following, then. And they must have known there was no escape for me in this corner.

Desperately, I felt my way along the wall. Something was propped against it – an iron frame of some sort. Discarded shelving from a kitchen or shop, firmly wedged against the wall. I grasped hold of it and started to climb. A sharp edge caught at the skirt of my dress, and I heard it rip. Bother. The shelves bowed under my weight and for a moment I feared they would give way, but they held. I scrambled to the top and heaved myself up onto the wall.

I could see the tops of their heads now – two men, both muffled up with hats pulled low. Like the man in the car that had driven into Mrs Jameson in Fitzroy Square.

I swung my legs over the wall and looked down the other side. I had no idea what was below me, or how far the drop was. But I could hear the men's breathing, coming harsh with the fog. One hacked a cough, then spat. They weren't trying to be quiet.

'Where's she gone?' muttered one. 'There's no way out from here.'

I thought of screaming for help. But the girls in Great Windmill Street, the men looking for whatever they hoped to find there – they wouldn't help me. And my pursuers would find my escape route, soon enough.

I eased myself to the edge and dropped into the darkness.

The shock of the fall took the breath out of me for a moment. I landed on my hands and knees, hitting cobblestones and mud. Bright eyes darted away, rats or mice heading back into their lairs.

'She's gone over the wall,' shouted one of the men, his voice rough but somehow familiar. I struggled to my feet, my knees bruised and sore. Now where?

I'd dropped my handbag in the fall. I felt around on the ground for it, then heard them climbing up the shelving. Deciding discretion was the better part of valour, I ran again.

They caught me where the alleyway took a sharp right turn. I'd run blindly into the bricks, and they ran straight into me, the impact knocking the air from my lungs.

One of them took hold of my coat lapels and heaved me to my feet. It was too dark to make out his features. He smelled of cheap tobacco and beer. And a faint, incongruous whiff of lilac.

Chapter 33

'Let me go,' I said, deciding to get my attack in first. 'The police know I'm here. They'll be along any minute.' If only, I thought. I'd have given anything to see Inspector Chadwick come round that corner with a couple of handy constables.

'Liar,' said the rough voice. 'You've been warned to keep your nose out. You and that Yankee woman. You should have listened.' He took hold of my chin. 'Shouldn't you?'

I knew who this was, now. The smell of lilac from his mother's bedroom, the familiar voice. He must be wearing her scarf, the dark blue paisley I'd noticed before. I wondered how long he'd been following me. Was it him driving the car that almost killed us in Fitzroy Square?

'Stop it, Mr Norris. We're trying to help find your mother's killer,' I began.

'She knows you,' said the other man. His voice was reedy with a slight wheeze. 'What are you going to do?'

'Shut up,' growled Norris. 'Now, where's those papers you took from the house?'

'What papers?'

His fist thumped into my jaw, snapping my head back. I gasped in shock. No-one had ever hit me before. Not on purpose, anyway. Not since play fights in the nursery with my

161

brother. The shock almost took away the pain, although that arrived a second later.

'I don't have them,' I gabbled. 'I haven't even looked at them, Mr Norris. Honestly.' Thank heavens I had remembered to drop them off before I came out.

His face was very close to mine. I could smell the tobacco and beer on his breath as he leaned in.

'Liar.'

I felt him shift his stance to hit me again, and twisted rapidly, ducking my head. His fist grazed the wall behind me, and he grunted in pain.

I shoved him away as hard as I could and tried to escape under his arm. His companion took hold of my hair and yanked my head back. I shrieked. We struggled in the darkness, none of us able to see what we were doing. My hand curled around his scarf and I pulled, trying to get his face away from mine.

'You're going to have to do her in,' the thin-voiced man said, breathless with panic. 'She can identify us.'

'I won't,' I said. 'Honest. I'll say I didn't know who it was. Just someone who attacked me in the dark.' It had been a mistake to let them know I recognised Norris, I realised.

'Shut up!' he roared. I kicked out frantically, trying to trip him. The other man came at me from the side, and I jerked my elbow, feeling satisfaction as I made contact with his face. He shouted in pain, a high-pitched whine.

Just faintly, I heard music, as if a door had opened.

'Help me!' I shouted, putting as much force as I could into my voice. 'Over here!'

Norris slammed his weight into me again, flattening me against the wall.

'Now, where are those papers?' he asked.

If I was just fighting one of them, I thought, I might have a chance.

'My handbag,' I said. 'I dropped it when I came off the wall. It's back there. The papers are inside.'

'Go and get it,' he said to his companion. I heard the man run to do his bidding.

'Can't leave you to tell tales, though,' he said. 'That's what happens if you go wandering these streets at night on your own. They probably won't find you for a day or two. And who's to say that it wasn't a business arrangement gone wrong?'

He took his scarf in both hands and pressed it to my neck. I felt my throat close as I struggled frantically to loosen its pressure, tried to gather my remaining strength for one last effort. Was this it? I thought sorrowfully of my parents, already grieving the loss of one child. What on earth would they make of this shameful death?

Chapter 34

Norris fell backwards without a sound, releasing my neck. I doubled over, gasping as the breath came back.

'Quickly. Get up. Can't hold him for long,' came a woman's voice. I heard his breathing, heavy but muffled.

'Here, grab my hand.' Another woman reached down to me. I grabbed, and she hauled me to my feet.

'Hey,' shouted Norris's mate. 'What's going on?'

'Blimey, Frankie. There's two of them. We'd better leg it.'

We legged. I could hear Norris groaning.

'Where?' I gasped.

'Down the steps,' called my saviour, tugging me along by the hand. A glow of lights and blare of music came from a basement ahead of us. Someone stuck their head up from the stairwell, silhouetted against the glare.

'What's happening? Frankie, I don't want trouble.'

'Let us in, QV. Quick as you like.'

We rattled down the metal stairs. A heavy green velvet curtain was pulled aside. The door was slammed shut and firmly locked behind us.

'Now, what's all this? She looks like a budgerigar that's been in a scrap with a tomcat.' A tall, regal woman in an old-fashioned evening dress of black bombazine and a widow's lace cap looked at me in disdain. Her voice was a refined contralto, her face handsome and imperious.

I looked down at my torn lilac dress, filthy shoes, and ripped stockings.

'I'm sorry,' I said. Then I looked at my two rescuers. The one called Frankie wore breeches, lace-up boots and a waistcoat over a white shirt, her dark hair cropped short as a man's. She was very young – maybe seventeen or eighteen – and a wide grin split her face.

'We couldn't leave her out with those blooming thugs, now, could we? Come on. Admit she's pretty.'

The other girl, the one who'd hauled me up from the ground, was equally young. She had a snub nose, freckles and soft brown curls tied at the nape of her neck. Her loose green tunic dress had a patch of mud where she'd knelt to help me.

'I'm Lily Rose,' she said. 'This is Frankie, and this here is Queen Vic, who runs the club. What's your name?'

'Marjorie,' I said. 'Thank you so much. I think the two of you probably saved my life.'

She looked pleased. 'Frankie's the one,' she said. 'We just popped out for a moment and heard you yelling. She's done the training, see. Her auntie was a suffragette. I'm going to do it next. Jiu-jitsu. Japanese, you know.'

The woman they called Queen Vic was still staring at me. 'I can't have you in here looking like that, Marjorie,' she said. 'You'd better go through to the office and get yourself fixed up. Lily Rose, you go with her. Frankie, get a couple of the fellows to go with you and see if those ruffians have cleared out. I don't want my customers being assaulted before they even get here.'

I followed Lily Rose into a side room, where the music was

165

quieter. A few mismatched armchairs clustered around a low table. Tucked into one corner was a sink, next to a dressing table covered in bottles, pots, and tubes.

'What is this place?' I asked.

'Don't you know?' Lily Rose looked surprised. 'This is Caravanserai. I thought you must have been looking for us. Not many people come down Ham Yard otherwise. Not if they know what's good for them.'

She ran water into the sink. 'Blimey, you did take a pasting. You've got blood on your face. I'll stick the kettle on.'

Caravanserai. I don't know what I'd been expecting, but it wasn't this cosy room with a big brown teapot and a rag rug on the floor. But this was the office, I reminded myself. Maybe the dancefloor would be a terrifying pit of iniquity.

'Thank you.' I looked in the mirror and pulled a face. My lip had split, and blood was smeared across my mouth. My eye-black had run down my cheeks, and my hair was all over the place. I realised I was shivering and sat on the wooden chair in front of the dressing table, pulling my muddied coat around me.

There was something in my hand. I unclenched my fist and opened my fingers. It was a scrap of fabric, dark blue with a paisley pattern. I raised it to my nose and smelled the lilac scent. I must have torn it from Norris in the struggle.

'We need to call the police,' I said.

'No, we don't,' said Lily Rose.

'But I've got evidence. I know who it was, and they're probably still around here somewhere. They might catch them…'

'Listen, duck.' She put a mug of hot tea in my hand and crouched down before me. 'I know you've had a shock. But no-one calls the police to Caravanserai. We'd all be arrested, and Queen Vic would be prosecuted for running an immoral establishment. It'd close down for good. You and me and all the girls would get felt up or worse by the coppers taking us in. You don't want to know what would happen to the boys. I'm sorry you got attacked and all, but you don't bring the police to this door. Understood?'

I was silent. I'd been brought up to trust the police, but then I'd never been on the wrong side of them. I thought about Inspector Chadwick, and the nice Constable Yates. Would they really behave in such a way? Right or wrong, Lily Rose and her friends had rescued me. I couldn't get them in trouble.

'Understood. Sorry.'

She beamed. 'Atta girl.'

I washed my face and began untangling my bird's-nest hair with a comb. There wasn't much to be done with my shoes, but I could probably manage a temporary repair to the rip in my skirt.

'Have you got a needle and thread?' I asked.

She found a sewing kit under the dressing table and passed it to me. 'What were you doing in Ham Yard, then?' she asked. 'If you weren't looking for us.'

My hands were shaking too hard to thread the needle. She took it from me, threaded it and passed it back.

'Actually, I was,' I admitted. 'I just didn't know I'd found you. I didn't know what the club looked like, and I got lost in the backstreets. Then I realised those men were following me, and I panicked. I climbed over a wall at the end of the alleyway, but they caught me.'

She nodded. 'Lucky for you that me and Frankie heard. There're often some dodgy characters hanging around here.

167

How did you hear about us? People don't usually come on their own. Not first time, anyway.'

I remembered the story I'd planned to tell. 'A friend of mine from the Slade Art School. Hugh Williams? He's a tutor there. He told me about it, said I should come along. He comes here quite often.'

She laughed, her eyes lighting up merrily. 'Hugh? He's a one, isn't he? What, so you're a model? Do you pose for the life drawing? I've thought about doing that. Don't you get cold?'

'Oh, it's all right. They have a fire going,' I said. 'You get used to it.' I wondered if that was true. I couldn't imagine stripping off my clothes and standing in the middle of a room, all those people staring at me. 'You know Hugh, then?'

She opened her eyes wide. 'Everyone knows Hugh. There, you're looking better already. Use a bit of Queen Vic's war-paint if you like. She keeps it out for anyone who needs to glam up when they arrive.'

Cautiously, I re-applied eye-black and a touch of pink on my swollen lips, then twisted my hair up into a pleat.

'Very pretty,' she said. 'You ought to get it cut, though.'

I smiled. 'So people keep telling me. But what if you change your mind? It'd take ages to grow again.'

She laughed and opened a cupboard. 'You can always fake it.'

A whole row of wigs hung from pegs – auburn ringlets, blonde plaits, a jet-black geometric style like the pictures of Cleopatra. They must have masquerade balls, I thought. I loved a bit of dressing-up.

'Come on,' she said. 'I don't know about you, but I need something stronger than tea after all that.'

'Oh!' I stopped in dismay. 'I lost my handbag. I haven't got any money.'

She shrugged. 'I'll stand you a drink.'

'It's me that should be buying,' I said. 'After all you've done to help.'

She turned her grin on me again. 'You can owe me one. You'll have to come back now, won't you?'

She led me out into the hallway, then through another green velvet curtain.

Chapter 35

Beyond the curtain, the lights were dim and the music loud. Jazz played from a gramophone – not ragtime, like Freddie and his friends had played at the Italian Roof Gardens, but a cool-toned, languorous sound that felt almost hypnotic. It was hot and airless from the crush of so many people crammed in together.

As my eyes got used to the semi-darkness, I saw people dancing, swaying to the rhythm in close embraces. There were no chairs, but divans were placed around the dancefloor, draped with scarlet and black Indian dhurries. Men in all manner of outfits, from full evening dress to working attire, lounged on them against big tasselled cushions. Low brass tables held red glass lanterns glowing with candle flames. The walls were hung with curtains of black fabric. It felt like being in an enormous tent in the desert.

People were smoking, drinking, and talking. In the darker corners, couples held hands and kissed. Possibly more; I didn't like to look. I glanced again at the dancefloor. Men danced with men, women with women. Bust to bust, like learning to waltz at school. I tried not to stare at the two men closest to me, immaculately dressed in white ties and tailcoats, gazing into each other's eyes.

Along one wall, a draped trestle table served as the bar. A man wearing a tasselled cap and velvet smoking jacket asked what we wanted.

'Two bottles of Best,' said Lily Rose. She turned to me. 'That all right for you?'

'Yes, thank you.'

Frankie strolled up to us. 'Don't I get one?'

'Make that three, Dennis.'

We plumped down on the nearest divan and Frankie got out a packet of Woodbines.

'Go on, then. Tell us all about yourself,' she said, lighting up.

'Marjorie's a model at the Slade School,' said Lily Rose. 'She works with Hugh Williams.'

Frankie narrowed her eyes and blew out smoke. 'Do you, now?'

'He told me about Caravanserai,' I said. 'He said he was here on Thursday night, with one of the Slade students. Ralph Garrett, his friend. Do you remember?'

She took a swig of beer. 'Any particular reason why I should?' She took Lily Rose's hand, a possessive gesture. Were they a couple? I wondered, fascinated. I'd heard of women like that, of course, but I'd imagined tragic old maids with moustaches and cats, not these lively young women.

'Well, there was a murder that night,' I said. 'And Ralph's been pinched for it. But if he was here, he couldn't have done it, could he?'

'Oh, my goodness,' said Lily Rose. 'I heard about that. Ralph's a lord or something, isn't he?'

'His brother is,' I said, recognising a desire for aristocratic gossip. 'The fourth Baron Bessborough. He owns a huge estate in Suffolk. Ralph's the younger brother, though, so he's an

171

Hon, not a Lord. That's what Hugh says, anyway.'

Frankie shook her head. 'Load of blooming nonsense. They'll be first up against the wall, come the revolution.'

I looked at her in surprise. 'What revolution?'

Lily Rose grinned. 'Frankie's a Bolshevik,' she said. 'Don't mind her.'

Frankie leaned forward, hands on her knees. 'Listen, Marjorie. We're not too keen on people coming round here asking questions. There was a bloke in last night, too, wanting to know about Hugh and whether anyone would vouch for him.'

'Was there?' I thought for a moment. 'What did he look like? Was he wearing a paisley-patterned scarf?'

'I said, we don't like questions. And I know most of the girls who model at the Slade. I've never seen you hanging out with them. What's your game, eh?'

I felt bad for trying to deceive them when they'd rescued me at their own risk. Perhaps it would have been better to be straight from the start.

'The thing is, I do know Hugh,' I said. 'He did tell me about this place. And that he and Ralph were here on Thursday, but that he couldn't tell anyone. He said he couldn't ask anyone here to stand up in court and swear to an alibi, and that he'd lose his job and get Ralph into trouble. So, I came here to try to find out for myself.'

Frankie was leaning back, one eyebrow cocked, her boot resting on one knee. She looked rather dashing.

'I've been investigating the murder, you see. With my boss. She's a detective,' I admitted.

'Police?' asked Frankie, drawing her brows together.

'No! No, she's independent.' I didn't like the look she was

giving me. She'd clenched her fists and looked ready to throw me out. 'Like Sherlock Holmes. She investigates things to make sure the wrong people don't get pinched for them. We don't need anyone to swear to anything. We just need to find out who really did it – but we can't do that unless we can rule out Ralph and Hugh.'

Lily Rose looked cross. 'You said you was a model!' She seemed quite disappointed.

'I didn't, actually. I just told you I knew Hugh from the Slade,' I reminded her. 'It was you who thought I was a model. Although I admit I went along with it.'

'Who were those blokes knocking you about outside, then?' asked Frankie, still suspicious. 'What've they got to do with all this?'

'One of them was Mrs Norris's son,' I said. 'The woman who got murdered. We've been trying to talk to people who we think might have reason to want Mrs Norris dead. And he didn't seem to like it. He was trying to get hold of something I found at his house, some papers that she'd hidden. But I didn't have them on me, thank goodness.'

I wondered if Norris and his mate had found my handbag. It contained my pocketbook with all my notes about the suspects, as well as my money.

'She was blackmailing people, wasn't she?' said Frankie. 'Hugh told me. There's more than one Caravanserai customer who will be glad to see the back of Betty Norris.'

Goodness, I thought. A whole new set of suspects. Would we ever get to the truth of this case?

'I think you'd better talk to Queen Vic. She can decide what to do with you. But don't give her no nonsense. She'll see right through you, and you'll be out in Ham Yard on your tod, with no-one coming to help no matter how loud you scream. Got it?'

Frankie and Lily Rose escorted me back to the office, where Queen Vic was sitting in one of the armchairs with her feet up, counting cash.

'Now then,' she said. 'What's all this about?'

I thought back to my conversation with Hugh that morning. It seemed like days ago. But he'd said he talked to the woman running the club on Thursday night, while he was waiting for Ralph to arrive. Maybe she would remember, if I could persuade her to talk to me.

I decided to take Frankie's advice. I began at the beginning, with meeting Hugh, Ralph, and Mrs Norris at the dinner party in Mecklenburgh Square. I told her about seeing Betty Norris's body the next morning, and how Mrs Jameson had been engaged to investigate the murder. I explained how we knew about the blackmail, and that we were trying to find the real killer.

'The thing is, I'm pretty sure that Hugh was telling the truth. Ralph isn't the murderer, and nor is he. But unless I can be absolutely sure, we don't know who to rule out. All I want to know is, *was* Hugh telling the truth? He said he'd talked to you on Thursday night, and that you'd offered to introduce him to a party from a musical show, but then Ralph arrived. That would have been about quarter to one. Does that sound right to you?'

Queen Vic had listened without comment, her sharp eyes showing she was following my every word.

'Betty Norris was a menace,' she said finally, her voice sombre. 'But she was a businesswoman. She knew the risks she was taking. We had an arrangement. She got a regular cut of the takings, and she left me alone.' She smiled, in a not particularly nice way. 'The same sort of arrangement I have with some of the police officers you're so friendly with, dear. What happened to Betty Norris wasn't right, although I won't pretend I'm sorry she's dead. But I don't want my customers caught up in the police investigation.'

'I understand,' I said. 'This is between us. But Hugh and Ralph already are caught up, aren't they? I just want to make sure that poor Ralph doesn't hang for what someone else did.'

She nodded. 'I suppose he might decide to tell the police where he was, eventually. Maybe you can prevent it from coming to that. So yes, young lady. Hugh and Ralph were here on Thursday night, like you said. Hugh from half past midnight and Ralph maybe quarter of an hour later. They stayed till we closed, around three. But I'm not planning to stand up in court and swear to that, and nor are my customers.'

I felt enormously relieved. 'Thank you. I know you have to be discreet.' I thought about what the girls had told me. 'There was someone in here yesterday asking about Hugh, Frankie said. Do you know who it was?'

She looked thoughtful. 'I hadn't seen him before. He didn't fit with our usual types. He was a common sort of chap, for all his smart suit and trilby hat. It was odd. He said he'd heard Hugh might have been in on Thursday, and he wanted to know if anyone remembered. But he wasn't like you, dear. He seemed almost to hope that no-one did.

'And then he started making veiled threats – saying that we needed to keep our mouths shut if Hugh had been here, because he knew people in high places who could get us shut down. Well, I slung him out after that. No-one told him anything, I don't think.'

Common, with a smart suit. I didn't suppose Royston Norris had a smart suit. Would Reginald Clegg count as common? My mother would probably think so. 'Was he dark-haired and rather handsome?' I thought about how Mum had described Clegg. 'A bit of a ladies' man.'

Queen Vic shook her head decisively. 'No. He wasn't a looker. He had a thin face, a shifty look about him. Smoked foul-smelling tobacco that he rolled himself. And his voice was pure south London.'

'Oh dear,' I said, smiling. 'Like mine?'

She laughed. 'No, you talk beautifully, dear. You've had proper lessons, haven't you? Now, I think we'd better get you safely home. I'll get a couple of my burlier gentlemen to take you back to Piccadilly and put you in a taxi. Don't want you getting in any more trouble on your way.'

Chapter 36

I was exhausted by the time the taxi pulled up outside The Ritz. Only two weeks ago, I'd been almost too nervous to walk through these doors, yet now it felt like home.

'Blimey, Miss Swallow,' said Jim, the night doorman. 'Whatever's happened to you? Mrs Jameson's been that worried. She's had that policeman over, and everyone's been out looking for you.'

'Oh, dear.' I looked down at my filthy shoes. 'I don't want to muddy the carpet, Jim. Could you get rid of these for me?'

I padded down the corridor to the suite in my stockinged feet. If only I could just roll into bed and sort it all out tomorrow. But Inspector Chadwick and Mrs Jameson were waiting up like outraged parents. They pounced the minute I opened the door.

'Good grief, Marjorie, where have you been? You frightened the life out of me,' Mrs Jameson began. I walked into the light. 'Oh! Your face… you're hurt.'

Inspector Chadwick looked horrified at my ragged shoeless appearance. 'What on earth have you been up to?'

'I'm quite all right.' I touched my finger to the tender bruise on my jaw. 'I've found out where Hugh and Ralph were on Thursday night. I spoke to someone who saw them there.

Hugh arrived at twelve-thirty and Ralph fifteen minutes later and they stayed until three o'clock. They can't have murdered Mrs Norris. They went to a club, near Piccadilly. But I can't tell you which one. I promised not to.'

'I can guess,' said Inspector Chadwick, looking thunderous. 'And they treated you like this? My God, I'll have that place closed down so fast…'

'No!' I was horrified. 'No, the people in the club were lovely. They rescued me. They looked after me and made sure I got back safely. The owner even lent me the money for a taxi. I lost my handbag when the men attacked me in the alley.'

'Wait,' said Mrs Jameson. 'What men? Sit down, dear girl. Start at the beginning. Inspector Chadwick swears he put you safely into a taxi outside the Criterion at ten o'clock. What happened next?'

I recounted my story of getting lost and realising I was being followed down the alleyways of Soho.

'Good grief, Miss Swallow. I wouldn't send a police constable down there on his own,' said Inspector Chadwick. 'I can't believe you were so foolhardy.'

'I climbed over a wall,' I said. 'Trying to get away. That's how I tore my dress. But then they caught me, and one of them tried to strangle me.' I paused, shuddering to remember how close I'd come to death. 'But two girls from the club came and fought them off. One of them knew that martial art that the Suffragettes used to do. Then they took me to the club and helped me get cleaned up. And that's when I found out about Hugh and Ralph.'

'Jiu-jitsu,' said Mrs Jameson. 'I learned it myself. Thank goodness they were there. We'll have to get you lessons.'

'I'm afraid the men may have my bag, though, with all my

notes in it. I'm sorry, Mrs Jameson. But at least the dossier is safe.'

She shook her head. 'I'm just thankful you're safe. What would I have told your parents? Peter, we must find whoever was responsible. It might be the same people who drove the car at me.'

'Oh,' I said. 'I know who it was.' I'd forgotten to tell them. I dug in my coat pocket for the scrap of fabric. 'Here. His scarf tore while we were struggling. It was Royston Norris, Mrs Norris's son.'

Inspector Chadwick jumped up and took it from me. 'Why didn't you say so?' He ran to the door. 'I'll put the word out. We'll have them under arrest by the morning.'

I sank back into my chair. 'Will he let Ralph go now?'

Mrs Jameson poured me a glass of brandy from the bottle on the table beside her sofa. 'I don't know. Peter was about to order Hugh's arrest when I called him at midnight wanting to know if he'd kidnapped you. He came straight over here when I said you hadn't returned.'

Of course. He'd been on his way to the Café Royal when I left him at Piccadilly Circus. He must have found out that Hugh's alibi wouldn't wash. I took a mouthful of brandy, its warmth coursing through me.

'But he won't arrest Hugh now?' I asked.

Mrs Jameson shrugged. 'The trouble is, we only have your word for it that someone at a club you won't name told you they were there on Thursday night. It's not exactly evidence, Marjorie.'

I flopped back, exhausted. All that effort and danger, and I hadn't even helped to get two innocent men off the hook.

'I promised the people at the club not to tell the police,' I said.

'But I didn't promise not to tell you. It's called Caravanserai. It's in Ham Yard. Queen Vic, who runs it, said the police know about it, but they usually give them warning when there's going to be a raid. She pays them, Mrs Jameson.'

She didn't look as shocked about this evidence of police corruption as I'd been myself.

'I suppose it's illegal. A club for homosexual men,' she said. 'And women, too?'

I nodded. 'But they were really nice to me,' I said, earnestly. I thought again of Lily Rose, helping me sew up the rip in my dress, and buying me a drink. Queen Vic, getting two of the men to escort me into a taxi, and lending me the money. Frankie, with her dashing air and challenging eye, who'd fought off Royston Norris. I'd have to find a way to pay them back.

'I should hope so too. I'm amazed you went on your own. Did Hugh tell you about the club?'

I nodded, then bit my lip. 'But he told me not to tell anyone. I promised. So, I thought I'd go and find out for myself.'

Mrs Jameson was looking thoughtful. 'You really are turning into an excellent asset, Marjorie. But you mustn't put yourself in danger like this. Now, I'm sorry to be tiresome, but I will need your help getting off this sofa and into my bed. I sent the nurse home this evening – I couldn't bear any more of her sanctimonious ways. We'll talk more in the morning.'

Chapter 37

I fell into my own bed minutes after helping Mrs Jameson into hers, barely able to keep my eyes open. It seemed only moments later that I woke, stiff and sore, to a maid bringing in tea.

'Good morning, Miss. Shall I open the curtains? Mrs Jameson wants to know what you'd like for breakfast.'

I glanced at the clock by my bedside. It was past nine o'clock already.

'Gosh, is that the time? I'll be through in a minute. I'd better have a quick wash.' My stomach rumbled. 'I don't suppose there's bacon?'

Mrs Jameson was sitting at the writing desk enthroned in a new wheeled chair, its woven cane back fanning out like a peacock's tail. She looked better than yesterday. She was always pale, but what colour she had was back in her cheeks and her eyes were bright. The nurse hovered in the background in a spotless white apron and cap.

'There you are, dear. Graham will be up with breakfast in a moment. How are you feeling today? Nurse Barrington, could you take a look at Marjorie's face? It's rather bruised.'

I felt pretty wretched, but I didn't want to worry her. My jaw throbbed, the grazes on my hands and knees stung and my head ached. This latter could have been down to the brandy that Mrs Jameson had pressed on me before bed. Or, I supposed, the beer at Caravanserai, or the wine at the Italian Roof Gardens. Goodness. What a night.

Nurse Barrington tied on a face mask and grasped my chin, none too gently. 'She's fine,' she said. I submitted to having my wounds dabbed with disinfectant. The iodine made them sting more. The nurse tutted at my winces.

Bacon and eggs worked their usual magic, though, along with a pot of tea and a few rounds of toast and marmalade.

'That's better,' I pronounced. 'Is there any news from the Inspector?'

'He telephoned half an hour ago. They still haven't found Norris and his mate. The house in Sidmouth Street is under surveillance, but I don't suppose he will go back. Which means that you and I will need to be very careful, Marjorie. I won't have you gadding around London on your own until they are safely under police guard.'

I sighed. Perhaps that would be for the best. And I could catch up on Mrs Jameson's correspondence. The house agency had sent over some new particulars.

'It's Sunday, remember?' said Mrs Jameson. 'Why don't you go home? They might be under lock and key by tomorrow. I'd be happy to send you home in a taxicab, for security. I don't suppose Norris would go looking for you in Catford.' I looked up quickly, to see if Mrs Jameson was laughing at me. She wasn't. But Nurse Barrington was looking down her nose, the snooty madam.

I thought about it. Sunday was always a sad, quiet day at home. My mother would be on her knees in church and my father on his knees at the allotment, each trying to make sense of their world. Then we would have Sunday lunch, with an empty chair staring gloomily at us as we chewed our way through boiled bacon. It wasn't my favourite day, but I'd had enough excitement for the week.

'Perhaps that would be a good idea,' I said. 'If we can find a taxi prepared to go all the way to south London.'

South London. There was something nagging at my memory. What was it?

Chapter 38

My mother was pleased to see me, at any rate. She fussed over my bruised face, exclaimed at my ripped lavender frock, and lamented with me about the ruined shoes. I told her that I'd tripped getting out of a taxi and fallen in the gutter. I wondered what she would say if she knew how I'd really come by my injuries. As it was, she was content with tutting at my clumsiness.

'If there's a wrong way to do it, you'll find it. Here, give me that needle. You're all fingers and thumbs.'

I handed it over. My mother was an excellent seamstress. After my adventures of the past few days, it was quite nice to be looked after.

Dad came home from the allotment with a basin of late raspberries and three enormous marrows. Mum pounced on the former and rolled her eyes at the latter. The allotment was an erratic source of fruit and vegetables, but it seemed to produce a never-ending stream of marrows every autumn. I tried not to turn my nose up at the big watery chunks of it when they reappeared alongside the bacon for Sunday lunch. I mustn't get too used to chicken escalope and strawberry ice-cream, I told myself.

After we'd eaten, Dad sat in the front room with the

newspaper, snoring. As Mum and I washed up, she brought me up to date with the church gossip: a litany of mild scandal about the new vicar's changes to Evensong, grievances about the cleaning rota, and deaths of people I might have met once, many years ago. I felt the familiar impatience, the stultifying gloom of a Sunday afternoon with nothing to do. I wondered what was happening in town. Had Royston Norris been arrested yet? Was Ralph still in custody? Had Mrs Jameson lost her patience and thrown Nurse Barrington out of The Ritz?

I was thankful when I heard a smart rap on the door knocker. 'I'll get it.' I unlatched the door.

'Hullo. I thought you might like to go for a walk.'

It was Freddie Gillespie, his fair hair plastered down and his face Sunday-clean, clutching a bunch of pink and white chrysanthemums. It took me about three seconds to get my coat and hat.

We walked past the closed shops and the picture palace on Rushey Green and through the familiar streets of terraced houses, the yellow London brick warmed by the afternoon sun. Privet hedges and shrubs crowded the little front gardens. Eventually we came out into Ladywell Recreation Ground. I stretched out my arms and spun around, enjoying the feeling of space. I felt like I hadn't breathed properly in ages.

'Glad to be home?' asked Freddie.

I smiled. 'Sort of. It's nice to be somewhere you can relax. But it's not what you call exciting, is it?'

He looked understanding. 'I know. At least you've got green space here. In Brixton, I can walk for ages and not see a blade of grass. But there's plenty of life. And that's the main thing, isn't it?'

185

I considered him again. His sandy hair had flopped forward, softening the white shrapnel scar that ran from the corner of his eye. His face had lost the pinched, anxious look it'd had just a couple of weeks ago. His new job must be suiting him.

'You look happy, Freddie,' I told him.

He laughed, picked up a stone and spun it into the stream which ran through the park.

'I suppose I am. It's the band, you see. I like playing with people. It's more fun than playing on my own. When it's just you, you're worried all the time about hitting a duff note. When there's five of you, especially playing jazz, it's all about the way you sound together. And if you make a mistake, they just laugh and weave it in.'

'And do you play every night at the Italian Roof Gardens?'

'No, three nights a week. Thursday to Saturday. On Wednesday night we have a regular set in a night-club in Soho. I prefer that, really. People come who know about jazz, who want to listen to the music and dance. At the Roof Gardens, it's just rich people showing off, shouting and laughing over the band. Or investigating murders. Have you found out who did it, yet?'

I smiled. 'Not exactly.' I told him about my expedition into the nightlife of Soho the previous evening.

'Good grief.' His smile had gone. 'I wish I'd known what you were planning. I wouldn't have let you go on your own. I'm amazed that policeman did,' he said, chucking another stone.

'He didn't know,' I admitted. 'I gave him the slip after he put me into a taxi.'

He shook his head, but his blue eyes were twinkling. 'Evading the police. Visiting illegal drinking dens. Does your mother know what you do for a living, Miss Swallow?'

'No, and I'd thank you not to tell her,' I said. 'She's very impressed that I have a nice respectable job as a lady's secretary.'

'You should come and see us play at The Harlequin. T-bone would be particularly pleased to see you. I think he was quite smitten. Which reminds me. We talked to Reg, the doorman, after the Criterion shut up shop last night.'

We had crossed onto one of the rustic bridges that spanned the river. The water was low, trickling over the pebbles. A discarded beer bottle was lodged in the reeds.

'Go on, then.'

'T-bone asked him about that party you showed us the picture of. Reg said the chap gave him a big tip when he called the taxi, later. But he remembered him slipping out just before one o'clock. He went over to Eros in the middle of the circus, where the flower sellers sit. Now, Reg reckoned he was there to meet a girl because that's what these chaps do. So, he watched, and he was having a bit of a laugh at his expense, because it looked like he'd been stood up. He lit a cigar, and he kept looking at his pocket watch and walking back and forward.

'Reg said this went on for about twenty minutes, and it looked like your chap had had enough. He'd chucked his cigar and was walking back to the Criterion when someone came running up from a side-street and yelled at him to stop.

'He stopped, and they hurried away together, down towards Jermyn Street. Then a couple of minutes later, your man ran back, alone, and into the Criterion.'

'Hmm.' I dropped a pebble into the water and watched it ripple. 'Interesting. I wonder who the man was. I don't suppose your Reg could describe him? Was he wearing a paisley-print scarf, for example?'

'Don't know about that. Reg said he was wearing a long coat and had a trilby pulled down over his face, with a muffler wrapped around. He didn't get that close a look at him.'

A trilby. Didn't the man who'd been at Caravanserai wear a trilby, too? The one with the south London accent. I remembered I hadn't told Mrs Jameson about him.

I glanced at my watch. Perhaps I should go back tonight, after all.

Chapter 39

At nine o'clock on Sunday evening, I let myself quietly back into the suite, thinking that Mrs Jameson might be sleeping. My mother had been disappointed that I wouldn't stay the night. She'd asked if I was too grand for my own bed in Catford, now I was used to The Ritz Hotel. I tried to explain that I needed to be with my employer. I'd felt uneasy about leaving her alone with only Nurse Barrington for company. And I wanted to tell her about the mysterious man with the south London accent who Reginald Clegg had met on the night of the murder.

I placed my overnight bag on the floor. The lamps were off in the empty drawing room. I reached for the switch, then paused. Something felt wrong.

I waited, my nerves on full alert. A dim light came from the windows overlooking Green Park, where streetlamps glowed. As my eyes got used to the gloom, I could see papers strewn across the desk by the window, its drawers pulled open. More papers lay on the floor around the desk. Mrs Jameson was not careless with paperwork. Even if she left it for me to file, she always kept the papers in order.

The desk had been ransacked.

I eased off my outdoor shoes and tiptoed silently across

the room on the thick carpet. My room too had been visited; the sheets and blankets were rumpled and pulled back, the wardrobe and drawers open.

There was no sign in the drawing room of Mrs Jameson. Her empty wheeled chair stood beside the door to her bedroom. I approached it, my heart thumping. There was a light showing under the door. I waited, listened. What had happened to her? Had the burglar harmed her?

Relieved, I realised I could hear breathing. But it was heavier than usual. I heard a snort, then a snore. There was another noise, too. Scratching, clicking. A slightly wheezy sigh, which did not come from the person asleep.

Someone was in there with Mrs Jameson. I thought of calling down to reception for help. But what if that came too late? I imagined a knife pressed to her sleeping throat; a pillow held over her face.

I pushed open the door. Nurse Barrington knelt on the floor in front of the open wardrobe, turning the dial of the room safe. She looked at me, her mouth open in dismay, then sprang to her feet.

'What on earth are you doing?' I asked.

She swallowed, then tried to bluff. 'Mrs Jameson asked me to take out her cheque book. She wanted to pay me for some things she'd asked me to bring her,' she said.

The cheque book was kept in the desk drawer, not the safe. It was probably somewhere on the drawing room floor.

I crossed the room to Mrs Jameson's side. She lay on her back, her hair wrapped in a chiffon scarf, her fine cambric nightdress buttoned to the neck. She was breathing heavily with her mouth open, snoring. She had not stirred at our voices.

A glass stood on the bedside table, with white residue in the bottom. I shook her shoulder.

'Mrs Jameson? Can you hear me?' No response. Her head lolled sideways, then rolled back. She'd been drugged.

I glared at the nurse. 'What have you done to her?'

'I gave her a sleeping draught. She was in pain and needed to rest. Really, Miss Swallow, if you are going to throw accusations around, one of us will have to give notice,' she said.

It was then that I recognised her voice. It was low-pitched for a woman, but would be slightly reedy for a man. I looked more closely at her face. There was the shadow of a bruise, a mark that would be missed if you weren't looking for it close-up – or if she'd been wearing a mask, as she had this morning. Covering up the place where I had elbowed her in the face, in a dark alley in Soho late on Saturday night.

Nurse Barrington was Royston Norris's partner in crime. And she'd been alone with Mrs Jameson all day.

I backed towards the door, got the doorknob in my hand. I needed to get her away from Mrs Jameson.

'That's all right, then,' I said, forcing a smile. 'Don't get into a tizzy about it. She doesn't keep the chequebook in the safe. It's in the writing desk drawer. Couldn't you find it when you were looking earlier?'

She looked wary, but relieved. 'Everything was such a mess,' she said. 'It looked like she'd been pulling out all of her correspondence.'

'Oh, yes,' I said. 'She does that. Why don't we have a proper look? We don't want to disturb Mrs Jameson. Like you said, she needs her rest.'

Reluctantly, Barrington followed me out of the door. I

191

snapped the light on in the drawing room.

'She really did make a mess, didn't she?' I said, brightly.

I went over to the desk and started picking up the papers. I saw the chequebook and nudged it under a pile with my foot.

She crossed the room to stand beside me. She was much taller than me, and no doubt stronger. She loomed over me, deliberately intimidating.

'A word of advice, if I may. I think you should be very careful, Miss Swallow. I looked at some of those papers, while I was searching for the chequebook. I wonder if you know what sort of woman you're working with.'

I certainly know what sort of man you're working with, I thought. How on earth did she get mixed up with Royston Norris?

I laughed. 'I'm quite capable of looking after myself, thank you. And now I remember why you couldn't find the chequebook. It's in my room, over there.' I pointed with one hand, while my fist closed around my room key with the other. If I could just get her inside, I could slam the door and lock her in, then call the police.

'Maybe you should go and get it, then,' she said, not moving.

'Come and help me look.' I started to feel desperate.

'Oh, I don't want to intrude into your private room, Miss Swallow,' she said. 'I'm sure you understand.'

We stood facing each other. My plan was clearly not going to work. I needed to try something new.

'How do you know Royston Norris?' I asked.

She didn't hesitate. Her big hands grabbed around my waist, and she lifted me off the ground. I flew across the room and landed heavily on the sofa, thankful for a soft landing on its heaped cushions.

'Keep your nose out,' she hissed. 'Or you'll both regret it.'

She was out of the door before I had time to recover.

I jumped up and grabbed the telephone. It took me a few seconds to realise that she'd taken the precaution of cutting through the wire. By the time I'd run down to the reception hall, Barrington was gone.

'What's happening?' asked Jim, as I pushed out of the door. 'That nurse woman just shot out of here like a rat up a drainpipe.'

'Where?' I asked, breathless.

'Down Arlington Street. What's happened – has she nicked something?'

'I found her trying to get into the safe. I need to know where she goes.'

'Wait.' He grabbed my arm. 'You can't go out without your shoes.' He called inside to one of the uniformed luggage boys. 'Charley, come quick. You know that Nurse Barrington? She went that way. Follow her and see where she goes. Keep back, though. Don't let her see you. And Sidney? Call the police.'

Sidney, the boy on reception, picked up a telephone on the desk. 'Scotland Yard, please, operator. Yes, the usual extension.' He grinned at me. 'You and your boss don't half make my job more interesting, Miss.'

'Thanks, Sid. And can you send the doctor up to have a look at Mrs Jameson? She's asleep, and that woman gave her something to knock her out.'

We waited anxiously for Charley to come back, his shiny shoes muddy.

'She went up St James Street, round into St James Place then through the tunnel into Green Park,' he said, puffing. 'Doubled back to the taxi rank on Piccadilly and jumped into a cab there.

I've got the number, Miss.' He proffered a scrap of paper.

'Oh, well done,' I said. 'You're a proper detective, you are.' He blushed with pleasure.

Inspector Chadwick arrived barely half an hour after Sidney had called him. The hotel doctor emerged from Mrs Jameson's room with his black bag.

'Nothing to worry about,' he said. 'It's just a sleeping draught, as she said. Stronger than I would advise, but it will do her no harm. Now, how about you, Miss Swallow? Are you injured?'

I shook my head. 'I'm quite all right. I'm sorry we're giving you so much trouble, Dr Moss.'

He smiled. 'It all adds variety,' he said. 'I'll sit with her for a while, just to be sure.'

Relieved, I explained to Inspector Chadwick what had happened. 'I realised she was Norris's companion from last night,' I said. 'She's tall, so I thought she was a man when she was wearing men's clothes. Then I recognised her voice and saw the bruise where I'd thumped her.

'She must have thought I had the dossier in my handbag last night. I suppose that's why they followed me after I left The Criterion – to try and get it back. Then when they realised I didn't have it, they thought it must be in the room safe.

'Nurse Barrington expected me to be out all night because Mrs Jameson told me to go home, so she took the chance to drug her and try to crack the safe. Fortunately, I'd used the hotel strong room.'

'But how did she come to be here at all?' asked the inspector. 'She could have killed Iris at any time.'

I thought for a moment.

'There was a nurse at the hospital. She recommended her. And I suppose…'

He grabbed his hat. 'The hospital nurse must have been the one to deliver the anonymous letter on behalf of Royston Norris. Right, Miss Swallow. I have work to do. Don't let anyone into the suite unless you know them.'

'Wait,' I said. 'She took a cab. This is the registration number. That might be a quicker way to find her.' I waved Charley's scrap of paper. 'The doctor is sitting with Mrs Jameson. Can't I come with you? How are you going to recognise the hospital nurse without me, anyway?'

He took it, his face breaking into a grin. 'If we ever open a women's criminal investigation department at Scotland Yard, Miss Swallow, I'm putting you in charge.'

Chapter 40

Constable Yates was waiting in a police motor car down Arlington Street. 'Hop in, Miss. You joining us, then?'

'Miss Swallow has provided very useful information,' said Inspector Chadwick. 'Now, take us to the taxi rank on Piccadilly.'

I waited in the car while he spoke to the drivers of the vehicles on the rank and showed them Charley's paper. They pointed him to the green-timbered cabbies' shelter, next to the Green Park railings. He disappeared inside for a few moments, then emerged.

'I've spoken to her driver,' he said. 'He dropped her on the Euston Road, just before St Pancras station. She didn't go into the station, though. She crossed over to Judd Street and he picked up a fare at the station, then came back here. We don't know exactly where she went. I think we'd better take a detour to the University College Hospital and see if we can find this nurse.'

We drove through the Sunday-quiet streets to the hospital. I'd tried and failed to remember the name of the nurse who recommended Nurse Barrington, although I felt sure I would recognise her. Inspector Chadwick strode through the red-brick entrance and down the carbolic-scented corridors to find someone in charge. I followed on behind with Constable Yates. In the matron's office, a harassed-looking woman in her middle years went through a big logbook to see which nurses had been working on which shifts.

'There we are, Inspector. Three nurses attended Mrs Jameson during her stay. One of them, Jane Wright, is on duty now. Follow me, and I will ask if she can help you.'

In the end, it hardly mattered whether I recognised her. Nurse Wright looked up from the drugs trolley she was stocking, saw me flanked by two policemen and gave an enormous start. Then she abandoned the trolley and ran off down the corridor.

'Nurse! Stand still,' called the matron, sharply. The nurse stopped, perhaps trained too well to ignore the voice of authority. She turned slowly, and tears were already on her face.

Sitting in the matron's office, she admitted it all. She'd been friendly with Nurse Barrington, who she had known under the name of Maureen Philps. They'd kept in touch, even after Nurse Philps had been dismissed for petty theft from patients' lockers.

'We used to go to the pictures on our day off,' Jane said. 'She always treated me. And her young man came along sometimes and took us out to tea.'

'What young man?' I asked.

'His name's Roy. Roy Norris. You probably know about what happened to his mother. He was right cut up about it, Maureen said. She was out of her mind with worry about him.

'On Friday evening, she called for me at the nurses' lodgings. She told me about poor Roy's mum and said that someone he blamed for her death was in the hospital. She asked if I knew about a Mrs Jameson, who'd come in after a motor car accident. She said that she was a relative of Mrs Norris and stood to get money from her death.

'I agreed to deliver a letter. I mean, there's nothing wrong with that, is there? And then she said that I should recommend her for a private nurse, if one should be needed, using a different name. And I did that too.'

She looked from one to the other of us. 'I'm sorry if it was wrong. But there was nothing wrong with her nursing, was there? I don't see what else I could have done.'

Inspector Chadwick sighed. 'You've been very helpful, Nurse Wright. Now, can you tell us where Nurse Barrington – Maureen Philps – lives? I'm sure that will help us even more. We may not need to pursue other charges against you.'

We came out of the hospital with Maureen Philps' address: Flaxman Court in Flaxman Terrace, just along from Judd Street where the taxi driver dropped her off.

'And it's barely five minutes' walk from Sidmouth Street, where the Norrises lived,' observed Inspector Chadwick. 'Looks like the beggar has been lying low right under our noses.'

We headed along the Euston Road as fast as Constable Yates could drive. Minutes later we were making our way up the stairwells of the red-brick block of dwellings in Flaxman Street. Inspector Chadwick banged on the door of a flat on the third floor.

'Police! Open up.'

The door stayed shut. Constable Yates was preparing to put his shoulder to it when the next door along swung open.

'No point in yelling,' said a pinched-faced woman in a shawl, leaning in the doorway with a baby in her arms. 'You've missed her. She grabbed her stuff and did a flit, not quarter of an hour ago.' She pointed her foot at the mat. 'Key's under there. Try and keep it down; I've just got this one off to sleep.'

Deflated, we let ourselves into the apartment. It was almost bare. The drawers were open and half-empty, the nurse's uniform abandoned on a chair. Inspector Chadwick pulled open the wardrobe. A couple of men's shirts hung in it, one larger than the other. There was a skirt and dress, a pair of women's shoes, and a crumpled pair of trousers.

'Look! My handbag.' I pounced on it and turned it out. The money was still in my purse, but the pocketbook was gone.

'Norris has been here, all right,' said the inspector. He held up a scarf, in dark blue paisley print. 'The question is, where is he now?'

Where would they go? He'd stayed close to his home, up to now. His mother owned property all over Bloomsbury, I remembered. Maybe there was an empty house he would head for. But if he hadn't gone there already, perhaps he needed to collect the keys.

'How well guarded is the house on Sidmouth Street?' I asked. 'It backs onto the park.'

'We've got someone at the front. He keeps an eye on the alleyway,' said the Inspector. 'But you're right. It might be worth taking another look.'

'Wait,' I said. 'There's more than one entrance to the park, isn't there? Let's go round the Mecklenburgh Square side and walk through.' The same walk Mrs Norris had taken on her way home from the party.

Could she have been murdered by her own son? It seemed unnatural, but if Norris was prepared to strangle me and run over Mrs Jameson, he was obviously capable of it.

We parked in Heathcote Street and went through the black wrought-iron gates. The gardens were even more gloomy in the dark; the tombs loomed from the shadowy corners, and I imagined villains lurking behind every shrub. We stepped softly, our eyes on the Norris house on the other side of the park, a bulky dark silhouette against the sky.

'No signs of life,' murmured Constable Yates, his voice low.

I scanned around the gardens, glad of the policemen to my left and right. Something caught the corner of my eye. I paused, trying to think what I'd seen. A point of light, there and gone.

'Wait,' I said. 'I saw something.'

We stood still. It had been over to the left, at the far end of the gardens towards the Foundling Hospital. I saw it again, a tiny point of orange light. A cigarette end, glowing briefly as someone drew on it. I tugged Inspector Chadwick's sleeve and pointed. It came again and went.

We withdrew to the cover of the wall.

'There's someone by the old chapel of rest,' said Inspector Chadwick. 'Excellent work, Miss Swallow, but now I need you out of the way. Please don't argue – I can't worry about you while we do this. Stay here. Yates, you go round the left wall. I'll cross and approach from the other side.'

I was disappointed to be dismissed, but I could see his point. I shrank against the wall and tried to penetrate the darkness with my eyes as the policemen approached the chapel of rest from both sides.

I didn't have to wait long.

I heard a sudden outburst of shouting, then Constable Yates's whistle. Someone came running across the lawn, heading for the exit where I waited. The figure was muffled up, with a trilby hat pulled low over his brow.

I pulled a dead branch from the bush next to me. As the figure approached, another in hot pursuit behind, I threw it across the gravel path. The figure stumbled, swore, and staggered. Seconds later, he was brought down by a handy rugby tackle. Constable Yates quickly overpowered him and snapped handcuffs onto his wrists, behind his back.

Constable Yates grinned at me. 'Good work, Miss,' he said.

Royston Norris looked up, saw me, and spat.

A moment later, we were joined by Inspector Chadwick and Nurse Barrington, also handcuffed. She looked at me in contempt.

'You'll wish you'd listened to me,' she said. 'One day.'

Chapter 41

'This one looks quite good,' I said, turning over a sheaf of photographs from a house agency. 'It's in Bedford Square. Shall I telephone and arrange a viewing appointment?'

I was tidying up the paperwork that had been strewn around Mrs Jameson's room. I'd found a whole heap of unopened house details, including these from an agency recommended by Eileen Power, which had its headquarters in Bloomsbury.

'Yes, if you like.' Mrs Jameson had been grumpy all morning. She was extremely annoyed to have been taken in by the Barrington woman and had a headache from the strong sedative. I suspected she was also frustrated not to be able to get out and investigate with me and Inspector Chadwick. I'd brought her up to date with everything that had happened while she'd been out for the count the night before.

She seemed to have lost interest in the house hunt, with all the excitement of the investigation. But there was something about the photographs of this house I liked. Perhaps it was the pots of geraniums on the windowsills and in front of the door. They made it look friendlier than the grand mansions of Mayfair. The rooms looked modern and comfortable too, not stuffy and formal. I made a note to call the agency.

Inspector Chadwick had telephoned first thing in the morning to ask after Mrs Jameson's health and brief us on the latest news. Norris had refused to tell the police a single thing, except for steadfastly denying that he had anything to do with his mother's death. But the police had found a car that he kept in an old mews off Judd Street, and it looked to be the one that had hit Mrs Jameson. They had also found my pocketbook in his jacket. He must have intended to continue the family business. No wonder he didn't want us visiting all of the blackmail victims and stirring things up.

Nurse Barrington had admitted only that she'd offered her services to Mrs Jameson on Norris's request. She'd said she was trying to help him recover his property, illegally abducted from his house by me.

Mrs Jameson was deep in the illegally abducted dossier.

'As we thought,' she said, looking up. 'Mrs Norris had a list of dates and times that Reginald Clegg visited his wife's sister in the six months before his wife's unfortunate accident.' She smiled the feline smile that meant she'd found something out. 'And not just that. There's a letter from Clegg to Lydia, dated four days before Moira's death. Listen:

'"My dearest girl, it's all set. Get out of town on Sunday. Visit your country cousins or something. If Moira asks you to come with us to Richmond, for heaven's sake make an excuse. Trust in me, dearest girl. Fortune favours the brave." Well, I can imagine the police would be interested in that.'

'Good gracious,' I said. 'They must really have wanted Mrs Norris out of the way. Will you give it to the inspector?'

She looked a lot more cheerful. 'I certainly will. It may not be enough to convict Clegg of his wife's murder, but it should certainly prompt some awkward questions. That ghastly man deserves all that's coming to him.'

And so does that ghastly woman, I thought, remembering Lydia Clegg's chilling composure.

I realised that I hadn't told Mrs Jameson what I'd found out about Reginald Clegg's movements on the night of Mrs Norris's murder. Quickly, I filled her in.

'We know he went out from the Italian Roof Gardens at one o'clock, then came back half an hour later. But he couldn't have murdered Mrs Norris. The doorman was watching him the whole time. He waited for someone by the fountain in Piccadilly Circus.

'The doorman said he couldn't describe the man Clegg met, because he was wearing a long coat and had a trilby pulled down over his face, with a muffler wrapped around. Same as the man asking about Hugh in the club.'

'Interesting.' Mrs Jameson half-shut her eyes. 'Although trilby hats are ten-a-penny. Tell me more about the man in the club.'

I recited what Queen Vic had told me. 'She said he had a strong south London accent. And that he started making threats, saying he knew people in high places who could get Caravanserai closed down.'

'Hmm,' Mrs Jameson mused. 'It sounds like he was making sure Hugh didn't have a usable alibi. I mean, he would have known that no-one in the club would stand up in court and swear to it. So, perhaps Hugh was intended to be the fall guy.' I didn't know what that meant. 'The man he wanted to take the fall, take the rap,' said Mrs Jameson, her voice impatient. 'Trilby planned to frame Hugh for the murder.'

'Oh!' I said, light dawning. 'He wanted the police to think it was Hugh. Which was why he put Hugh's drawing in Mrs Norris's pocket. It wasn't intended to link to Ralph, after all.'

She threw me a sardonic glance. 'Finally. The question is, who was trying to frame Hugh? We know Reginald Clegg couldn't have cut Betty Norris's throat himself. But he has plenty of money. He'd be more than happy to pay to have her bumped off, as he put it, would he not? Perhaps the man he met at Piccadilly Circus was the murderer, reporting back after the deed was done. And perhaps Clegg was paying his fee.'

Of all the people we'd interviewed, Reginald Clegg was the one who seemed most capable of murder. But who had wielded the knife? My mind went to the man who had tried to strangle me in the alleyway.

'Should we tell the inspector?' I asked. 'Clegg might have been paying Royston Norris to kill his own mother. He'd have had time to get back to Sidmouth Street from Piccadilly Circus and raise the alarm at two o'clock.'

'We should certainly ask Peter to find out who Clegg met,' said Mrs Jameson. 'But Norris isn't from south London, is he? Perhaps you should have another chat with Hugh and find out if he knows Clegg. I've managed to restrain Peter from clapping Hugh in irons for giving a false alibi. But I can't guarantee how long that will last.'

I slit open the next envelope in the pile, written in a rounded girlish script.

'It's from Winifred Garrett at Bessborough Hall,' I reported.

'We haven't talked to her since Friday morning,' said Mrs Jameson. 'What does she say?'

I read the letter aloud.

Dear Mrs Jameson,

Please, please tell me if you have made progress in your investigation.

I am so worried about Ralph. Charles says the police have got it quite wrong and that he will bring it up in the House of Lords. But I worry that Ralph's nerves won't stand much more of being imprisoned.

You know that he was being blackmailed. Perhaps you do not yet know that this was because of his friendship with Hugh Williams. This has been misunderstood [this last word underlined several times]. *I believe he sees Mr Williams as a mentor and guide. I say this simply in the hope it may help your inquiries, for there has been enough speculation already. It is unpleasant, but I am informed that it is not uncommon among the household servants.*

I will try to return to London on Monday, although my brother would prefer me to stay here. Perhaps there is little I can do, but I hate to be so far away when poor Ralph is in trouble.

Yours sincerely,

Winifred Garrett

'There's not much new to go on there,' I said.

'Perhaps,' Mrs Jameson mused. 'She says that there has been speculation about her brother's relationship with Hugh Williams. It seems that their secret was not as well-kept as they thought. I wonder if anyone else knew that Ralph was being blackmailed.'

Chapter 42

The telephone rang. 'Visitor for Mrs Jameson,' said Sidney, from the reception desk. 'Lord Bessborough. Shall I send him up?'

The suite at the Ritz was large, but Lord Bessborough gave the impression of filling every corner. His man stood impassively by the door, as if he was guarding it.

'Well, Mrs Jameson? My brother has yet to be freed. And that Welshman remains at large despite, as I understand it, having given the police a false alibi. What have you done to earn my fee?'

How did he know about the false alibi? Perhaps his friends in the upper echelons of the Metropolitan Police had told him. No doubt they were making Inspector Chadwick's life even more difficult.

Mrs Jameson smiled imperturbably. 'Forgive me for not rising to greet you, Lord Bessborough. As you can see, I am indisposed. Would you like coffee? Marjorie will ring for some.'

He shook his head impatiently. 'I'm here for business. I have yet to receive any report of your progress. I am most dissatisfied.'

He sat down heavily in an upholstered armchair which

seemed to sag at his approach.

'I visited my brother yesterday, Mrs Jameson. He is in a state of nervous collapse.' His lip curled and I clearly saw his contempt for Ralph. 'I fear for the boy's life if he is not set at liberty. I repeat, what progress have you made?'

'We have been eliminating suspects,' said Mrs Jameson, her voice even. 'Mrs Norris had been blackmailing your brother, and many other people too. We have visited them and investigated their motives and alibis.'

'And?' he asked. He did not, I noticed, seem surprised at the news that his brother was being blackmailed.

'And we have eliminated most of them. Including, I should add, your brother and Mr Williams.'

'Dammit, woman. I know Ralph didn't do it. Why is he still in police custody, then?'

Mrs Jameson tapped her chin meditatively, always a sign of deep thought. 'I think we should have coffee,' she said. 'Marjorie, will you call for some?'

I picked up the telephone. 'Coffee for four,' I said.

'Of course. There's a lady at reception to see Mrs Jameson. Miss Winifred Garrett?'

I glanced at the awkward grouping. One more angry Bessborough sibling would not make much difference, I supposed.

'Send her up, please. And add another for coffee.'

Mrs Jameson gave Lord Bessborough her most charming smile.

'My Lord, I know where your brother was at the time of the murder. My intrepid assistant, Miss Swallow, has established that beyond doubt. Yet unless Ralph himself will admit to it, I cannot see the police accepting our evidence.'

'He'll do as I tell him,' said Lord Bessborough. 'Where was the boy? He should have been at home with his sister. I expressly told him as much.'

There was a discreet tap at the door and Graham arrived with the coffee. He set out five cups and saucers, coffee pot and cream, while Lord Bessborough tapped his foot in impatience.

'Shall I pour, Mrs Jameson, or will you serve yourselves?' Graham asked.

She smiled quizzically, indicating the cups. 'Are you joining us, Graham?'

He frowned, puzzled. 'I'm sure I was asked for five. But perhaps there was a mistake. I'll take one away.'

Another tap on the door. Lord Bessborough's manservant opened it. His eyebrows jumped to his hairline and a faint flush rose over his face.

'Oh... Jack.' Winifred Garrett rounded the door and saw us all watching. Her face was pink, and she seemed flustered. She wore a heather tweed travelling suit, with a most unbecoming hat jammed down over her ears.

'Thank you, Hudson.' She recovered her composure. 'Charles, I didn't know you were here. I came up by the morning train. I wanted to see Ralph and find out what was happening.'

'Dammit, Winifred. I told you to stay at home with Mother.' Lord Bessborough didn't seem to have much luck telling his siblings to stay at home.

Winifred set down her case and took a chair across the room from him. 'Well, I'm here now. I'm sorry to intrude, Mrs Jameson. I hoped you would have some news.'

Graham poured the coffee and made a discreet retreat.

'No intrusion, my dear. I was explaining to your brother

that I know Ralph did not kill Mrs Norris, and that he has an alibi. However, he must be brave enough to tell the police where he was.' She smiled at the girl. 'And I was about to add that I also know Hugh Williams cannot have killed Mrs Norris, because the two of them were together at the time, and probably for the rest of the night.'

Lord Bessborough jumped to his feet, knocking his coffee cup off the side table and onto the carpet.

'That's enough!' he shouted. 'I will not have my family dragged into the gutter with that – that sewer!'

We all stared at him. His face was the bright pink of boiled bacon. He snatched up his hat.

'Mrs Jameson, your contract is terminated. You will cease your investigations immediately. I can see that it was a mistake to bring in an American. You have no sense of propriety. And if you continue to make insinuations about my brother, expect to hear from my lawyers.

'Winifred, Hudson will take you back to Mayfair. I will ensure that Ralph is cleared of the accusations and slurs against him. Come.'

She shook her head, looking out of the suite window and over the trees of Green Park. 'No. I want to talk to Mrs Jameson. And then I'm going to see Ralph. I'll stay in my own house, in Doughty Street.'

Lord Bessborough stared at his sister for a minute, non-plussed. He didn't seem to know how to deal with such unexpected defiance. He leaned over her, put his puce face close to hers.

'If you do that, Winifred, I will terminate the lease on that house,' he hissed. 'I will cut off your allowance. You will stay where I wish and live how I wish. Expect that to be in Suffolk, with our mother. Is that really what you want?'

She said nothing, but folded her mouth closed. For a moment, I could see the resemblance between the siblings in the stubborn jut of their chins.

'Perhaps we should go, Sir,' said Hudson, Bessborough's man. My head jerked up at the sound of his voice.

Chapter 43

'He's hardly the only man to come from south London,' Winifred Garrett pointed out. 'I don't see why you should hold his origins against him. Especially as you evidently come from that direction yourself.'

As soon as Lord Bessborough and his manservant had gone, I pointed out the man's accent to Mrs Jameson, and asked Winifred Garrett about him. She looked rather heated, and her voice was defensive.

'Jack Hudson has been with Charles since the War,' she said. 'Charles trusts him absolutely. And so do I. He's a good man. He's devoted to our family.'

I sipped my coffee and wondered. She'd used his first name when she hadn't expected to see him. And she was rather too vehement in his defence. How close was their relationship?

'You said in your letter that someone in the household had told you there was gossip about Ralph's friendship with Hugh Williams.' Mrs Jameson slid the question in while I tried to look penitent. 'Was that someone Jack Hudson?'

She nodded. 'He thought I should know. That's what I mean. He cares about the family's reputation. He said he'd known Hugh in the army and that he was a bad sort. He was worried about Ralph, and about how it would look if people thought there was anything in the rumours.'

I remembered. 'Hugh told me he knew Hudson from Belgium,' I said. 'I'd forgotten.' He'd also told me that the man owed him money and was notorious for not paying his gambling debts, but it didn't seem the right time to mention that.

'And had you heard these rumours before Mr Hudson brought them to your attention, Winifred?' Mrs Jameson's voice was gentle.

She shook her head. 'I don't think so. Not about Hugh. But...' she set down her cup. 'But I'm not stupid, Mrs Jameson. I know my brother. He's not interested in girls. He never has been. I suppose... I suppose it wouldn't have mattered very much, in days gone by. He'd have married some equally clueless girl and they'd rub along together all right, and each have their own interests. Or he'd have just stayed a bachelor, kept quiet about it, and no-one would have cared.

'But nowadays, everything must be out in the open. Everyone's read Dr Freud, and people seem to want to talk about all sorts of dreadful things. It's all very well putting it in novels and calling it art. But this is real life, Mrs Jameson.'

My employer was watching keenly. I wondered if she too had picked up on the familiarity between Winifred and Charles Bessborough's manservant.

'I knew it would be difficult for Ralph when we got older. I thought it would be better if we were in London, away from Bessborough and Charles and all the things expected of us. And he was so happy, painting and learning and spending time with Hugh. I didn't believe there was anything really wrong about it. Until this happened.'

She burst into tears.

I'd tried to comfort her before and been rebuffed, so I left it to Mrs Jameson to pat her hand and pass handkerchiefs. Something was bothering me.

Why had Lord Bessborough not been startled to learn that Ralph was being blackmailed by Mrs Norris? Had Hudson told him? And had he warned Lord Bessborough about Hugh being a 'bad sort'? If he had warned Winifred, it seemed more than likely he had also spoken to his employer.

I sat down, slowly. Someone with a south London accent had been in Caravanserai on Friday, warning people not to say anything about Hugh's presence there on the night of the murder. And possibly the same man had been spotted in Piccadilly Circus within an hour of the murder, talking to Reginald Clegg. That, I admitted, was a connection I had yet to account for.

Hugh had said Jack Hudson was always in need of money. I thought of Mrs Jameson's motives for murder. Money, passion, revenge, and fear.

I felt sure there was something between Hudson and Winifred. I glanced at her now, sobbing messily into a handkerchief, and wished she would go away. I couldn't raise my concerns about the man who might be her lover with her sitting there.

'Why don't you go and talk to Ralph?' I asked. 'He's the only one who can sort out this muddle about the alibi, after all. I expect the police will release him once he admits to it.' I glanced at the clock. 'It's almost midday. You could see him at Bow Street now, then go back to Doughty Street to get ready for him coming home.'

She looked up, a little coolly. 'But I don't know where he really was. Do you?'

I hesitated. 'Yes, I do. He was in a club, with Hugh Williams. But he needs to tell you about it himself.'

She rose. Her pale blue eyes were cold, under reddened eyelids. 'I will go to him. I expect you to respect my confidentiality as a client, Miss Swallow. I do not expect to hear my brother's business spoken of outside of this room.'

I didn't like to remind her that her older brother had terminated our contract less than half an hour ago. Anyway, I just wanted her to leave.

Mrs Jameson waited until Winifred had closed the door behind her. 'Well, Marjorie,' she said. 'What did you want rid of her for?'

'There's something between her and that manservant, Hudson,' I said. 'Didn't you notice? She called him by his first name, when she came into the room and saw him unexpectedly.'

'I did,' said Mrs Jameson. 'Most suggestive. I also saw the way she looked at you when you mentioned his accent. She was most indignant. No-one likes reminding that their lover is common.'

I had more information. 'Hugh said that Hudson was always losing money at cards and still owed him five pounds. He said Hudson owed everyone money. Hudson might have gambling debts now. So, what if he was paid by the Cleggs to kill Mrs Norris? And then he tried to pin the blame on Hugh, because he knew from Winifred that they would both be at the party in Mecklenburgh Square?'

A slow smile spread over Mrs Jameson's face. 'You are learning fast, Marjorie. You won't need me to direct you, soon. Perhaps you should set up on your own.'

There was a slight edge to her voice, as if something had irritated her. I hoped she wasn't annoyed by my presumption.

I was learning all right, but I needed this job. I very much doubted I could earn five pounds a week and my board all-in as a private investigator.

'It's just a theory,' I said, humbly. 'What do you think?'

'It's a very good theory. Why don't you go up to The Slade and see if you can find out what else Hugh knows about Jack Hudson?'

I picked up my bag, then remembered. 'He won't be there. The school is closed on Mondays.'

She reached into her handbag. 'Here. Peter gave me Hugh's address. Apparently, he lives in a studio over a laundry in Caledonia Street, close by Kings Cross railway station. Most romantic. We are getting close, Marjorie. I can smell it.'

Chapter 44

The taxi drew up by the clutter of buildings that stood in front of the Kings Cross railway terminus, just as the clock on the tower showed twelve noon. The streets around were busy with taxis and goods vehicles. I made my way through the crowd of travellers clutching suitcases, past the tobacconists and offices of coal merchants and ticket sellers, and around the station for the underground railway.

I stood for a moment at the east side of the terminus, trying to get my bearings. A policeman stood like a sentry outside the station entrance, as the people swirled around him.

'Which way to Caledonia Street?' I asked.

He raised his eyebrows. 'What do you want there, Miss?'

'The laundry,' I told him.

He looked at my respectable but shabby coat. I was waiting for my first month's wages before I ordered the worsted for a new one. Presumably I looked reassuringly drab.

'Right you are. Go left at the corner and along York Way. Caledonia Street is the first turning on the right. There's a public house on the corner. The laundry is the next building along. Don't get them muddled, will you?' He gave me an avuncular smile.

One side of Caledonia Street was made up of small terraced

houses that gave straight onto the street. Young children sat on the doorsteps, trying to catch whatever scant beams of sun made it through the smoggy air. Coal dust from the nearby goods yards blackened everything – the bricks, the windows, the children's faces.

The Duke of York pub on the corner looked respectable enough. Just beyond it, Caledonia Steam Laundry was a rather grand-looking building in red brick with big arched windows and a white stone portico. I wondered how they managed to dry laundry without it getting dirtied with coal dust. A woman in a long apron was on her knees scrubbing the white stone doorstep at the arched entrance. The laundry at least was keen to keep up appearances.

'Hugh Williams? That artist fellow?' She sat back and looked me up and down, wiping her face. 'What, you one of those nude models, are you? How's the money? I bet it's better than this. I wouldn't mind giving it a go.'

I smiled. 'I'm not a model. I've got a message for him,' I said.

She pointed me to the second archway at the far end of the building. 'Go through there, and up the second set of stairs on your right. His studio's right at the top, fourth floor.'

I hurried along and started up the stairs. The deafening noise of the laundry – trolleys trundling across the floor, clattering and clanking of the steam washing machines, women's voices calling to each other over the din – came through the doors on each landing. It was hot; through the windows in the doors I glimpsed ranks of women lined up with ironing boards, their hair plastered down with sweat under their white caps. I didn't know what the rates of pay were, but it seemed to me they deserved a fortune for labouring in such conditions.

I was out of breath by the time I reached the final short set of steps to the top floor. They led to a curious sort of half-attic above the drying rooms where acres of linen hung on wooden horses. I paused to dab my face with a handkerchief; I was sweating almost as much as the ironing women.

The door was painted plain black, with a half-pane of frosted glass set into it. I could not see a doorbell or knocker, so tapped on the glass, wondering if Hugh would hear over the noise of the laundry. How did he manage to concentrate in these circumstances?

The door swung open at my touch. Beyond was a long, narrow room with arched windows all along the side, pale northern light washing through onto a faded parquet floor. Propped up in the middle of the room was a huge, astonishing canvas.

Hugh had said he didn't paint anymore; that he could think of nothing it was worth his while to paint. He'd been lying. I found myself drawn towards the canvas, despite a growing recognition of its horrors.

The jagged, ugly angles made me think of the Picasso exhibition. The painting was all black and white, disorientating and frightening. A skeleton wearing a tin hat rode straight at me on an emaciated horse. Its death's head grinned as it brandished a rifle, bayonet fixed. Death, the pale rider, moving through an exploded nightmare landscape of dead trees and barbed wire, monochrome under a full moon. With the background noise of the laundry downstairs, it seemed like a vision of hell.

I rounded the canvas and took in the rest of the room. There was a mattress on the floor, made up with grey blankets. On a plain table stood a whisky bottle and a glass, paper and pen.

There were two wooden chairs. In one sat Hugh, his mouth gagged with a twisted cotton handkerchief and his eyes pleading. Standing on the other side of the table with his back to me was a man in a long dark coat and a trilby hat. He was pointing a pistol at Hugh's head.

I screamed. The man swung around, and a shot whizzed past my head, the sound unbelievably loud in the confined space. I wish I could say I'd done something heroic – charged at him or run for help. But I simply froze in horror, unable to make a move of any sort.

It was Jack Hudson. He locked eyes with me for a long second and I saw him raise the pistol again.

'No!' I called, frantic. 'Please, Mr Hudson. Don't shoot.'

It wasn't a clever ploy, but I could think of nothing else to say. And it had the desired effect of making him hesitate.

'You shouldn't have come here,' he said. 'Now I've got no choice, have I?'

Pure south London.

'But you have, honestly,' I said. 'There's always a choice.' I grasped for anything to offer him. 'What about Winifred? You won't abandon her, surely?'

I risked a glance at Hugh. He was struggling against the ties that held his ankles to the chair. His hands were free, though. He was working at the knot that held his gag in place. Never mind that, I thought. Get your feet free and help me.

Hudson was staring at me. 'What're you babbling on about? What do you know about Miss Garrett?'

'She told us everything this morning,' I said, hoping wildly that my surmise was correct. 'She's crazy about you, Jack. She knows you're just trying to protect Ralph. Whatever's happened, whatever you've done, she'll still love you. She'll wait for you. So long as you don't make it worse.'

He shook his head slowly, a smile dawning on his face.

'Winifred Garret? You think I'm in love with that scrawny bluestocking?' He began to laugh. 'She has her uses, I admit. Keeps me up to date with their movements. But really. You women. Everything's got to be about you, hasn't it? Well, you've learned one thing today. It's really not.'

He raised the pistol again, taking aim more slowly this time. My knees started to tremble. How many shots in the barrel? Six, according to the detective stories I'd read. Five left to finish the job.

There was a crash and I dropped to the floor. I lay there a moment, heart thudding through my coat. No part of me seemed to be hit. But he still had four more shots.

'Get up, Marjorie! Now!'

Hugh's voice. I looked up.

Jack Hudson was on the floor, the remains of the whisky bottle shattered around his head. Hugh was leaning across the table, the broken end of the bottle still in his hand.

'Get his gun,' he shouted. 'And help me untie these ropes.'

I scrambled forward on all fours and grabbed the gun from Hudson's unresponsive hand. He was breathing heavily, his eyes closed but his eyelids starting to flicker. There was no time to waste.

'Quick. He's coming round.' I gave the gun to Hugh and crouched by his chair. The knots were tricky. 'Haven't you got a knife?' I asked.

'Over there. Canvas knife by the window,' he said.

I picked it up gingerly, recognising the style. It was the same as the knife that had been used on Mrs Norris – wickedly sharp. It sliced easily through the rope that held Hugh's legs.

He jumped up. 'Let's get out of here.'

Hudson was groaning. Hugh kept the gun trained on the

prone man until we were out of the door, then handed it to me to stow in my bag.

'I don't want to get pinched by the police with a gun,' he said. 'Come on.'

We ran down the stairs and into the street. Hugh pulled me by the hand past the staring woman scrubbing the steps and onto York Way, then whistled. One of the taxis that were lined up to wait for the train arrivals pulled away from the kerb and we jumped in.

'Take us to The Ritz,' I told the driver.

Chapter 45

Breathlessly, we explained to Mrs Jameson what had happened.

'I put you in danger,' she said, pressing her hand to her throat. 'Again. I am sorry. I never thought things would move so fast. Call for the inspector, Marjorie. If they're quick, they may catch him.'

I put through the now-regular call to Scotland Yard. 'He's not there,' I reported. 'He's gone to Bow Street police station. He must want to talk to Ralph Garrett.'

Mrs Jameson wheeled herself across the room and took the receiver. 'Hello? Mrs Iris Jameson speaking. Please convey a message to Inspector Chadwick immediately. Tell him it's extremely urgent. An armed man has attempted to shoot dead my secretary and is at large in the area of Kings Cross railway station.'

She gave Jack Hudson's name and description, as well as the address of Hugh's studio.

'And tell the inspector to put a watch on the home of Lord Bessborough, Hudson's employer. He may try to return there, or to the home of Miss Winifred Garrett, in Doughty Street.'

'He's not armed any more,' I said, opening my handbag. 'I took the gun.' I tipped it out on the coffee table. But I'd left the knife, I remembered. That had been stupid. If Hudson had murdered Betty Norris, he would be more than familiar with how to use it.

Mrs Jameson laid a napkin over the gun. 'We'll need to preserve it for fingerprints,' she said. 'Was Hudson wearing gloves?'

I couldn't remember. It had all been rather a blur.

'Yes,' said Hugh. 'Black leather gloves. He was going to kill me.' He'd spoken little since we arrived. He was shaking, his usual bonhomie drained away. He hunched forward on the sofa, his shirt open at the neck and his hair disordered. His eyes were quite frantic. I thought of the terrifying painting, and of the knife. Had I been wrong about Hugh all along? Surely not.

'He wanted me to sign a letter confessing to Betty Norris's murder,' he said. 'He made me drink whisky; forced it down my throat at gunpoint. I think the plan was to make it look like I'd confessed and shot myself in a fit of remorse.'

He reached out and clasped my hand. 'If Marjorie hadn't arrived when she did, I'd be dead.'

I jumped at the touch of his cold fingers. I reminded myself of all the reasons why I should not allow my heart to beat faster when he touched me. My heart ignored them and pattered away regardless.

'Well, I'd be dead if you hadn't coshed him with that bottle,' I said, placing his hand firmly back on the sofa arm. 'And you lied to me about your art. You are painting again. That canvas was extraordinary.'

He shrugged. 'No-one will want to see that stuff,' he said. 'They want to forget about the trenches. So do I, but it has to come out somewhere.'

'You were right, Marjorie,' said Mrs Jameson, respect in her voice. 'Your theory about Jack Hudson wanting to pin the blame for the murder on Hugh. Why do you think Hudson targeted you, Mr Williams? Marjorie said you knew him during the War. What happened?'

He shrugged. 'Nothing much. I didn't like him. He was sly. A bit of a bully. He'd watch for people's weaknesses, then pick away at them.' He sighed, dropped his head into his hands and spoke to the floor.

'He found out something about me and one of the men. Someone I was pally with, for a while. Hudson tried to get money out of us, to keep quiet. Like I said, he was always gambling and always broke. But then my pal got himself killed and even Hudson could see there was nothing doing there.'

The bitterness in his voice caught in my throat like London smog, acrid and thick.

Mrs Jameson's eyes were veiled, like a sleeping bird of prey.

'Have you ever heard of Reginald Clegg?' she asked. 'Do you know of any connection between him and Jack Hudson?'

Hugh sat up, looking puzzled. 'No. I mean, I've heard of him. That business with the boating accident was all over the newspapers. But I've never met the man. He wasn't in the army, was he?'

Mrs Jameson looked at me enquiringly. 'You said he had a wholesale business, Marjorie. Was he in a protected profession?'

I frowned. 'I suppose he must have been, because of supplying the troops with uniforms. His company had a big army contract that almost bankrupted them when the War Office said the goods were too shoddy to use.'

Hugh gave a harsh laugh. 'Must have been pretty rotten if

the army wouldn't have them. Half the time we got lumbered with boots that fell apart the first time you introduced them to mud, and jackets with the buttons held on by a thread. I thought it must have been Hudson, skimming the best stuff to sell on the side.'

Mrs Jameson's eyes snapped wide open. 'Hudson worked in the stores?'

He nodded. 'Not long after my pal died, he got transferred. I thought he must have had something over one of the officers, because he got a cushy quartermaster job back in headquarters. While we were stuck in the trenches, Hudson was counting socks and doling out tin hats. That's where he met Charles Garrett, I suppose. Garrett had a nice safe job in logistics, well behind the lines. Organised by his father, of course, who was Lord Bessborough at the time.'

Mrs Jameson wheeled herself to the window and looked over the treetops. 'So, Jack Hudson was involved with army supplies, at a time when Reginald Clegg was one of the main suppliers of uniforms? Hudson would have known the truth about the quality of the goods Clegg was supplying.'

'And he might have been involved in giving evidence for the army, after the war,' I added, excited. 'If Hugh's right and he was always in need of money, perhaps Reginald Clegg paid Hudson off. Perhaps that's why his company was able to settle with the War Office for less than expected. And Clegg knew Hudson as someone who would do anything for money.'

Hugh was looking from one to the other of us in astonishment. 'You do realise all of this is speculation, don't you?'

Mrs Jameson smiled. 'It's called deduction, young man. And Marjorie and I are getting rather good at it. However, there is one point I have yet to clear up in my mind. If Hudson was the murderer, why would Mrs Norris let him into the house?'

'Hell,' shouted Hugh. 'I should have thought of that. Because she knew him, of course. He fed her information, same as the rest of us. I'd always suspected he was the one who tipped her off about Ralph and me.

'The cold-hearted… he told her about Ralph so she could get her claws into the poor boy. And then I suppose he told his old pal Clegg that he could get rid of Betty, using information from Winifred about the party. He'd already got me lined up to frame as a suspect, because he knew I usually walked her home.'

The telephone rang and I sprang up to get it. 'Putting you through,' said Heidi. I heard with relief Inspector Chadwick's concerned tones.

'What in heaven's name have the two of you been up to this time, Marjorie?'

'Jack Hudson threatened to shoot Hugh at his studio in Caledonia Street. Then he tried to shoot me, but missed. Hugh coshed him and we left him on the floor, but he was coming round. If you're quick, you might find him,' I said.

'Right. Stay there, Marjorie. No more heroics. Tell me the full story later.'

The line went dead. Almost immediately I had replaced the receiver, it rang again. Heidi connected the call.

'Miss Swallow? Please convey a message to Mrs Jameson.' It was Winifred Garrett, her voice stiff.

'Of course. Is everything all right?' I wondered if she had somehow already heard about Hudson. I thought of the way he'd described her and felt rather sorry for her.

'I wanted to thank her for her help. The police are releasing Ralph from custody.' Despite her stiffness, I could hear happiness in her voice.

'Well, that is good news,' I said. 'Are you at the police station?' I wondered if she had seen Inspector Chadwick.

'No. I visited after I left you this morning. I must say, he was in an awful state, poor boy. Then I came back to Doughty Street. Charles telephoned a few minutes ago to say Ralph was being released, and he would go to collect him. I wanted to go too, but he told me to wait here and get some lunch ready. Ralph needs feeding up and looking after.' I wasn't sure I would rely on Winifred Garrett to feed anyone up, or indeed make them comfortable, but at least Ralph was out.

I replaced the receiver.

'That was Winifred. They've released Ralph,' I said. 'Isn't that good news? Charles is on his way to collect him now.'

'Thank goodness,' said Hugh. 'I must go round to see him. Poor boy: he isn't cut out for the rough stuff. I hope they haven't treated him too badly.'

Mrs Jameson looked up slowly from her chair. Her eyes were veiled, her lips moving slightly as if she was rehearsing an idea. Then she locked eyes with me and the veil was gone. Her eyes glittered, hard and bright.

'Marjorie, call down for a taxi to Bow Street. We have very little time. I fear Ralph Garrett is in extremely grave danger.'

Chapter 46

In the end, Hugh came with us in the taxicab, after stowing the wheelchair in the luggage space next to the driver.

'How are you going to get out at the other end, Mrs Jameson?' he asked. 'You can't expect poor Marjorie to carry you and that chair.'

I was relieved to have his company. Mrs Jameson had refused to tell me what had prompted our speedy exodus, repeating only that we must get to Ralph. The tendons on her neck stood out like taut cords and she leaned forward as if willing the taxi on through the crowded streets. The traffic was heavy at Piccadilly Circus, but finally the policeman on duty waved us across and we traversed Coventry Street and Leicester Fields. The cinemas and theatres whizzed by – the Alhambra, the Hippodrome, Wyndham's. The taxi driver, who'd been promised a hefty tip if he got us there quickly, shot across into Garrick Street and screeched left onto Floral Street before skidding to a halt beside the lofty heights of the wholesale flower market at Floral Hall.

'See if he's still there, Marjorie,' called Mrs Jameson. I jumped out of the taxi and ran across Bow Street to the police station. A constable stood at the bottom of the steps, between the lanterns.

'The magistrate court's round that side, Miss,' he said, pointing.

'I know. I'm here for the police station. I need to know if Ralph Garrett is still being held,' I asked, breathlessly.

He waved me in. I repeated my request to the sergeant at the desk. He was a big man, round of stomach, with a florid face and a walrus moustache. He leaned on the counter, and I could see he intended to take his time and no doubt amuse himself at my expense.

'We'll need to take down your particulars, Miss,' he said, looking me up and down. 'Why don't you take a seat over there and I'll see if I can find a lady officer to help you?'

'This is urgent,' I said. 'Is Inspector Chadwick still here? I spoke to him about a quarter of an hour ago.'

The inspector's name evidently gave him a jolt.

'Inspector Chadwick, eh? No, he left in a hurry. I can't help you there. You'll have to speak to Scotland Yard.'

I wanted to scream. 'I have. They told me he was here, and I spoke to him by telephone. But I need to know about Mr Garrett. Please. All I need to know is if he's still in the cells.'

He folded his arms. 'And what's it to you, Miss?'

I decided honesty was not the best policy. 'I'm Miss Winifred Garrett, Ralph's sister. I'm here to take him home to Doughty Street. I was told he was being released.'

He smiled, an unpleasant, leering smile. 'Well, you're too late, Miss Garrett. His Lordship was here before you. They left a couple of minutes ago, from the court side.'

I dashed back out and around the side of the building. Bow Street magistrates court and police station together made up a block of adjoining buildings and the court entrance was at the corner of Bow Street and Broad Court. It was often full of

230

people – supporters of those on trial, lawyers, policemen, the merely curious, and the press.

This Monday lunchtime, a crowd stood around the door waiting for the magistrates to rise. It included several press photographers with their big, heavy cameras.

'What's happening, Miss?' asked one of them as I raced to the corner. 'Have we missed something?'

'Did you see a man come out with another man?' I asked. 'Ralph Garrett, who was being held for the Sidmouth Street murder. His brother Lord Bessborough was supposed to be collecting him.'

'Yes, I got a nice shot of them coming down the steps,' he said. 'They didn't look very happy, considering they've let him out. Wouldn't tell us anything, would they, Bert?'

Bert, a young man with a notebook, shook his head. 'Blooming toffs. Never give you a word. What do you know about it, Miss?'

I decided to trade information. 'I've spoken to the police. Ralph Garrett has an alibi. There's another man under suspicion now,' I said. 'Still at large. Where did they go?'

Bert scribbled frantically in his notebook. 'Down towards Drury Lane,' he said, pointing. 'Thanks, Miss.'

I ran to the end of Broad Court, which connects Bow Street to Drury Lane. Lord Bessborough was helping his younger brother into the back of the big black Crossley motor car that I remembered from Mecklenburgh Square. Ralph looked thin and ill, as if he needed to be supported. Someone was in the front seat. I shaded my eyes to look.

I could hardly believe it. The man driving the car was Jack Hudson, currently being sought by half of the police officers in London. None of them seemed to have noticed the man sitting in the driving seat of a luxury motor car, just around the corner from the biggest police station in town.

I ran back to the taxi.

'Hudson's driving,' I gasped. 'Charles and Ralph are in the back. They're just setting off down Drury Lane, towards the river.' I stared at the empty driver's seat. 'Where on earth has he gone?'

'Call of nature,' said Hugh. 'I did ask him to wait.'

'We'll lose them,' said Mrs Jameson. 'Hugh, can you drive?'

'I never learned,' he said.

'I can,' I said.

Chapter 47

I'd never driven a taxi before, but I didn't suppose it could be any more difficult than an ambulance. I climbed into the driver's seat and looked anxiously at the gear levers. Fortunately, the man had left the motor running. I pressed down the pedal, disengaged the clutch and took off the hand brake.

'Hold on tight,' I said. The taxi gave a couple of enormous jerks, as if it was a horse trying to buck me off. Then I managed to get it properly into gear and we rolled away from the kerb towards the busy traffic of Bow Street.

I gave the horn a quick warning squeeze and nosed the taxi into the lines of vans and cars. I saw a double-decker omnibus bearing down on us and pressed my foot on the accelerator. We shot across the street, leaving the 'bus driver mouthing something extremely rude in our wake. The press photographers scattered as I rampaged down Broad Court. Stealing a taxicab right under the noses of the assembled police and magistrates was quite a way to start my criminal career.

At the end of the court, I paused and looked anxiously for the Crossley. I spotted it halfway down Drury Lane, hampered as much as we were by busy traffic. Hudson didn't know I was following, I remembered. All I had to do was keep the car in sight – and evade any pursuit when the taxi driver returned from whichever public house he had dropped into for his break.

'Well done, Marjorie,' said Hugh. 'You're doing grand.'

The traffic sped up as we passed the Peabody Buildings and the Theatre Royal. Scared of losing them, I squeezed us through a tiny gap between a baker's van and an enormous yellow Hispano Suiza, whose owner barely disguised his outrage at my cheek. I overtook again, until I was just two cars behind Lord Bessborough's Crossley.

The traffic slowed again as we approached Aldwych. Which direction would he take – left towards the City, or right along The Strand to Trafalgar Square? Neither direction, I reflected, would take him to Doughty Street. Whatever Winifred Garrett had been told, Charles was not taking Ralph home to Bloomsbury. Perhaps they would take him straight to Bessborough Court in Suffolk.

The Crossley merged into the stream of traffic heading east toward the Royal Courts of Justice. But instead of turning into Fleet Street, it pivoted sharp right so that we were heading west again along The Strand. I managed to yank the wheel around in time to follow the manoeuvre.

I kept close behind, hoping that Jack Hudson would not glance back and see that the taxicab behind him was being driven by a woman. A woman who he had narrowly missed shooting barely an hour ago.

I had assumed we were heading down to Trafalgar Square, but Hudson suddenly swung the car sharply to the left and plunged down a narrow street towards the Thames. I stood on the brake and threw the gear levers about, grinding down into second gear to take the corner. I clipped the kerb, even so, to the annoyance of a clutch of black-robed lawyers waiting to cross.

We passed a news boy putting up a placard on the corner. 'Latest: Baron's brother off the hook, police hunt new man,' it read. Bert had wasted no time in conveying my information to his newspaper. We passed a public house. To my right I glimpsed a green space and a Tudor building with big arched windows beyond.

'That's the old Savoy Chapel,' said Hugh. 'We're round the back of the Savoy Hotel.'

Ahead of me, the Crossley had turned right just past the chapel. At the end of the street, I could see the wide brown river.

I swung the taxi around the corner. The car turned left, then left again. We were in Savoy Place, a small garden shielding us from the rush of the Victoria Embankment. I stood on the brake pedal. The Crossley had stopped, pulled across the middle of the street to block it. The three men clambered from the vehicle, Charles supporting his younger brother. Where were they going? Somerset House?

'Quick. We mustn't lose them,' said Mrs Jameson. 'Curse this ankle. If you see a policeman, flag him down and get him to go with you. But keep your eyes on Ralph at all costs.'

I abandoned the taxi and ran with Hugh. The three men had reached the end of the street and turned right, towards the river again. By the time we reached the embankment, they had crossed the tramway and were climbing the steps up to Waterloo Bridge.

Chapter 48

We hurried up onto the bridge. A biting wind whipped along the river from the east, catching at our hats and swirling our coats about us. Upstream, the sun failed to break through the blanket of brown cloud that hung over Westminster. Traffic rumbled over the narrow roadway and the few pedestrians hurried along, heads down and collars up against the wind.

Ahead of us, the three men walked fast towards the middle of the bridge. Ralph was hatless, his overcoat flapping loose about him. His brother was next to him, holding his arm. Hudson had his hands in his coat pockets and walked behind them, glancing around every few seconds.

'He's going to see us,' I said, slipping behind a lamp post. 'We're close to the river police station on Waterloo Pier. Maybe we should ask them for help.'

'No time,' said Hugh. 'Look, they're stopping.'

I peeped out. The men had drawn aside from the pavement into one of the squared-off alcoves that sat on top of each of the bridge's piers. Ralph slumped forward, leaning his forearms on the parapet. I could not see his face, but his whole attitude expressed despair as he stared down at the water.

The Thames was flooding sea-wards. The river was high and full, the olive-green water churning and fast-flowing. Dread rose in my chest. I remembered what Hugh had said about Ralph; how he was more likely to injure himself than hurt another person. I thought of Winifred's fear that Ralph's nerves would not take much more strain.

His brother was still gripping his arm. Thank goodness, I thought; Charles would be able to prevent Ralph from doing anything silly. Then Charles brought out a paper from his coat pocket, holding it onto the edge of the parapet. He was urging Ralph to look at it, passing him a pen.

We were almost at the alcove now, half-running in our anxiety. Mrs Jameson had not told us what to do when we caught up with them. I supposed I would have to tell Lord Bessborough of his manservant's culpability. I only hoped he would believe me.

Hudson muttered something to his employer and both men turned to look sharply at us. Charles looked furious, but then he always did. Only Ralph Garrett seemed entirely oblivious to our approach.

'Lord Bessborough,' shouted Hugh. 'I know you don't like me, but listen. Your man is dangerous. He's a murderer. Keep him away from Ralph.'

Hudson suddenly took to his heels, dashing southwards across the bridge.

'Jack!' shouted Lord Bessborough. 'Stop, damn you.' But Hudson was not stopping for anyone.

I took a wary step towards the brothers. 'I believe Mr Hudson murdered Mrs Norris,' I said. 'He tried to frame Hugh Williams and was going to shoot him. He tried to shoot me. We were so worried he would do something to hurt Ralph. Thank goodness you're both safe. We need to find a policeman right away.'

Lord Bessborough stared at me in amazement. 'How extraordinary,' he said. 'Lucky you came along. Yes, that's clearly the thing to do. You two go down to the Thames Police station and get a policeman. I will stay here with Ralph, in case Hudson comes back.'

I should have been happy that he believed me. But it was all wrong. He should have shouted and blustered; told me I was an idiot. Then I'd have trusted him.

Ralph raised his head. His eyes were ringed with red, and he seemed hollowed-out with misery. He looked at Hugh.

'It's no good,' he told him. 'Can't you see that?'

He took the fountain pen from Charles's hand and scribbled his name on the paper, then dropped the pen over the parapet. He watched it spin down into the churning waters, then turned and thrust the paper at Charles, who took it and shoved it quickly into his pocket.

'There. Blame it on me. Blame it on Hudson, blame it on Hugh. So long as you survive, so long as the blessed house of Bessborough survives for another crummy generation.'

'What are you waiting for?' asked Lord Bessborough, irritably. 'Go on. You two go and get help. I'll look after my brother until you get back.'

'What was on that paper?' I asked. I thought of the 'confession' that Hudson had tried to get Hugh to sign.

'Nothing. Just a formality,' said Lord Bessborough. He didn't seem to have had much practice at lying. 'From the police station.' He glared at me aggressively, not loosening his grip on Ralph's arm.

I began to see what his plan had been.

'May I see it?' I asked.

'Certainly not. It's nothing to do with you,' said Lord

Bessborough. He turned to look again after Hudson, just in time to see the man disappear down the steps at the end of the bridge on the Southwark side.

Hugh gave me a wink and jerked his thumb over his shoulder. I looked behind him and saw three policemen running along the bridge towards us from the northern shore. Mrs Jameson must have managed to alert someone to come to our aid. Either that, or I was about to be arrested for stealing a taxicab.

Lord Bessborough looked back and saw them too.

'Splendid. Here we are,' he said. He was sweating, not in control for once. He dropped Ralph's arm and looked first one way, then another. The policemen were barely three hundred feet away.

'I'll follow Hudson, see if I can catch him,' he said. He started to run. I saw him reach into his coat pocket.

'Hugh!' I shouted. 'The paper!'

'I'll get the swine.' Hugh hared after him, light on his feet compared to the lumbering gait of Lord Bessborough, who was hampered by his long coat. Within a dozen paces he had caught him and grabbed his shoulder. But Lord Bessborough took the paper from his pocket, held it in the air. I cried out as it flew from his hand. The wind took it, high above our heads, and whisked it upstream.

Bessborough shoved Hugh towards the cars on the roadway and I gasped as he stumbled at the edge of the kerb. A boy on a delivery bike skidded to a halt.

'Watch where you're going,' he yelled. 'Blooming drunks!'

Hugh recovered his balance. He ran after Bessborough again, seized his coat collar and dragged him around.

'Ralph's worth two of you.' He swung a mighty punch that landed square on His Lordship's clean-shaven chin.

Bessborough grabbed Hugh as he fell and the two of them rolled over, struggling for supremacy. They looked like schoolboys, tussling in the gutter.

To my relief, a policeman rushed past me, blowing his whistle. I turned to Ralph. He was still staring into the water, seemingly unaware of the fight that had broken out just yards away.

'Ralph.' He looked up when I said his name. 'Why don't you come with me?' I wanted him off this bridge and away from the water. I'd seen the look in his eyes before among some of the more badly affected neurasthenics at the hospital. A haunted look, a look that said the burden they were carrying had become too much. The look of a man who could not see any further than ending the mental pain.

'No point,' he said. He put one knee on the parapet. My heart stood still.

'There is a point,' I said. 'I promise. There are good things to come, Ralph. The world is changing. Things will become easier.'

'My brother hates me,' he said. 'He wants me dead. Everyone hates me.' He sounded like a very small child, bullied and defenceless in a school dormitory, missing home. He scrambled up until he stood on the parapet, swaying in the wind. The wind that filled my ears, my mind, scoured through me.

'Your sister loves you. Winifred was so happy you were coming home. She would be very much hurt by your death. Hugh…' I hesitated. I wasn't sure that Hugh loved anyone, and I felt that nothing short of the truth would do. 'Hugh is very fond of you. He thinks you have great talent. And the world will love your paintings. You're only eighteen, Ralph. Please. Come down and talk to me.' I held out my hand, extending it slowly so as not to alarm him.

He looked away, up the river to where a few gleams of light touched the gilt on the top of the tower of Big Ben.

'I didn't kill her,' he said.

'I know. Nobody thinks you killed her,' I said. 'Things will be better, from now on. I promise. Everything is going to change.'

He turned his face back towards me. Streaks of tears ran from the corners of his eyes.

'Do you really believe that?' he asked.

'I do.'

I held my breath. He nodded and held out his hand towards me. I stepped forward and took his cold fingers. Then he looked down at the water below, and I saw him lose his nerve. He gasped and stumbled. He clutched at me. For a horrible moment, I thought he would fall and take me with him.

'There, now. Well done, young woman.' A policeman had us both in his arms and lifted Ralph down from the parapet. He handed him firmly into the grip of another policeman.

I buried my face in his navy serge coat, gasping for air. My legs didn't seem terribly reliable, and I wondered if I could sit down. Dimly I was aware of voices around us, exclaiming, shouting, calling. One voice in particular cut through the babble.

'Marjorie! Dear girl, are you all right?'

I looked up to see Mrs Jameson being wheeled at speed along the pavement by our taxi driver, his face a picture of confusion.

I nodded, but found I could not form any words.

Chapter 49

'What do you think?' asked Mrs Jameson. 'Of course, I will have my paintings and so on shipped over from Boston. That will make a difference. It's a little bare at present.' She stumped through the airy rooms, leaning on her black Malacca cane.

'I like it. Rather elegant; very modern,' said Eileen Power, pausing to admire the view out of the tall sash windows onto the plane trees of Bedford Square. The last of their tobacco-brown leaves were drifting to the ground.

The house had been owned by an American film producer and his English wife, and thoroughly modernised to their standards. A system of hot-air vents heated it from an enormous boiler in the basement, with no need for messy open fires. Despite the late-November chill, the rooms were cosy. We had already shown off the bathrooms – there were three – which would satisfy a Roman emperor with their luxurious plumbing and gold mosaic tiles. There was even a bathroom just for my use, adjoining my bedroom and sitting room at the top of the house.

We were in the large, bright drawing room, facing south across the square. The glass light shades on the walls were in the shape of scallops, against a pale green wallpaper with a trellis pattern. A fitted carpet of geometric design in green and cream covered the floor. Cream armchairs with green cushions, which had arrived that morning from Harrods, looked fresh and comfortable. A maid was watering a display of ferns on the console table.

'Good. I'm glad,' said Mrs Jameson. 'Now, let's have some coffee.'

I pressed an electric bell in the corner of the room. Minutes later, Graham Hargreaves appeared with a trolley laden with coffee pot, cups and saucers, and Mrs Jameson's favourite French macarons. I'm not sure how Mrs Jameson had persuaded him to abandon The Ritz to become her butler – or what she called her chief of staff – but I was awfully glad she had. We were still in the process of recruiting maids, a cook, a driver and all the other personnel that Mrs Jameson's establishment apparently required. Graham had quietly taken control and the house was already running tolerably smoothly.

We sat in the comfortable armchairs. 'Now, Iris,' said Eileen. 'I've had a letter from the south of France, from Winifred Garrett. She and Ralph have taken a house in Menton for the winter, to recover his health. And I read in the *Morning Post* that Lord Bessborough and his manservant are awaiting trial for murder. Explain, please.'

Mrs Jameson began her story. The police had picked up Jack Hudson as he tried to board a lighter at Grellier's Wharf, just south of Waterloo Bridge. The 'absolute loyalty' that Winifred had boasted of lasted about as long as it took the police to get him into a cell. Since then, he'd sought to blame the whole thing on his employer.

'He claims Lord Bessborough paid him to kill Mrs Norris, after Hudson warned Bessborough that Ralph was being blackmailed over his relationship with Hugh Williams. And that it was Bessborough's idea to pin the blame on Williams, to get rid of two birds with one stone. Lord Bessborough, on the other hand, maintains the murder was Hudson's idea all along and he knew nothing about it.'

'And what do you think?' asked Eileen.

'They're both thoroughly unpleasant characters. But I tend to believe Hudson. He had gambling debts. Why would he put himself at risk without financial gain? Lord Bessborough was horrified about the possible damage to the family name. So, he did what any right-thinking member of the British Establishment would do.' Mrs Jameson set down her coffee cup. 'He arranged to have a woman's throat cut, and to have an innocent man hanged for her murder. Except it didn't work out quite like that.'

'Thanks to you,' said Eileen, shaking her head in wonder.

'Thanks to Marjorie,' said Mrs Jameson, firmly. 'Her excellent detective work established Hugh's alibi. Of course, there was the stroke of luck that meant Hugh came with us in the taxi, instead of escorting Mrs Norris home as he usually did. And then there was Ralph's disobedience to his brother's instructions to remain at home with his sister after your party. Bessborough must have been horrified when Ralph was arrested and could give no alibi. That's why he engaged me to get Ralph off the hook. But he got more than he bargained for. When he realised, he sacked me and sent Hudson to force a confession from Hugh. And when Marjorie foiled that, he decided to sacrifice Ralph.'

The letter which Charles Bessborough had induced his brother to sign had disappeared into the churning waters of the river, but Ralph confirmed it had been a confession to the murder of Mrs Norris in a fit of madness. He had signed because he didn't much care what happened to him at the time.

'It was better, in Lord Bessborough's eyes, that his brother should die having confessed to being a lunatic and a killer, than live and be known to be homosexual,' said Mrs Jameson. 'I don't know what the English do to their boy-children at boarding schools, but I think it's about time it stopped.'

Eileen shuddered. 'Remove their hearts, poor things, I believe. But Hugh says the young people now are changing. And I see it myself in my students. There is more free-thinking, more willingness to question the values of their parents. What do you think, Marjorie?'

'I think it depends a lot on where you are,' I said. 'Most of my school friends are getting married, having children, doing exactly what their mothers were doing at their age.'

'But not you,' said Mrs Jameson.

I smiled. 'Not me. I think… after the War, it seemed terribly important to make the most of life. And perhaps we stopped believing that our parents were always right. They were tremendous supporters of the War when it started. And look how that turned out.'

Eileen looked kindly at me. 'Well, quite. I hope you do get to make the most of life, Marjorie. You should travel, you know. Visit places that are as different from here as you can imagine. India, China, Arabia. It will open your eyes.'

'I'd love to,' I said, politely. It had taken me almost twelve years to travel from Catford across the Thames into central London. I hadn't seen the sea until I was fourteen, when Dad took us to Margate one August bank holiday.

'We will certainly travel,' said Mrs Jameson. 'Next year, after we have this place sorted out to my satisfaction. Egypt, perhaps. I should be most interested to see the excavations that are being made around the pyramids.'

The pyramids. Just the thought of it made me dizzy.

'And what about the horrible man who tried to run you over, and strangle Marjorie?' asked Eileen, with a shudder.

'Betty Norris's son? He's facing a long jail sentence for blackmail and attempted murder,' said Mrs Jameson, biting into a raspberry macaron with relish. 'And that dreadful Nurse Barrington has been charged as an accessory.'

Reginald Clegg had told the police he had met Royston Norris in Piccadilly Circus on the night of Betty Norris's death. But it was nothing to do with the murder – he was paying Norris the monthly £200 blackmail money. Mrs Norris and Royston insisted on cash; Reginald Clegg insisted that the money should be handed over discreetly, well away from his home or business.

Clegg had tried to make himself seem like an innocent victim, but to my satisfaction, he and Lydia Clegg had both been arrested. The information we had uncovered in Mrs Norris's dossier meant the case had been reopened into Moira Clegg's 'accidental' death.

Graham came back with the morning post. Mrs Jameson looked it over and swiftly pocketed an envelope with an Italian post-mark and stamps, before passing the others to me. I sighed. I was no closer to finding out what had happened to Mrs Jameson in Rome. I opened the rest of the letters.

An invitation to the first night of a Christmas revue featuring Sarah Simpson and Bertie Post, who had recently become engaged to be married. I wondered what, if anything, Bertie knew about Sarah's son. Another card invited us to a private viewing of new paintings by Hugh Williams in January – his first exhibition for eight years. A scribbled note for me from

Freddie Gillespie, suggesting I should go to see him play with the All Stars at The Harlequin club in Soho.

And a letter from the American Ambassador to Great Britain, Henry Caldwell.

'I do hope you are recovered from your injury, dear Iris. Now, how about lunch? I'll come clean: I am in need of your deductive powers! As one compatriot to another, will you help me out of a scrape?'

I waved the paper at Mrs Jameson. 'Perhaps the pyramids will have to wait. We may have found our next case.'

* * *

Enjoyed Blackmail In Bloomsbury? Read the prequel for free.

So how did a nice girl like Marjorie Swallow end up working for a lady detective? And what happened during her interview for the job, in the Palm Court at the Ritz Hotel?

Subscribers to my Readers Club can download a free novella, *Murder At The Ritz*, which answers these questions and more! Readers Club members get a monthly newsletter with news about my books, events, special offers and promotions. Sign up at my website, annasayburnlane.com.

Notes and acknowledgements

Blackmail In Bloomsbury was inspired by classic British 'Golden Age' detective fiction of the 1920s and 1930s. I love reading these books by Agatha Christie, Dorothy L Sayers and Marjorie Allingham, although they are very much period pieces.

A more recent debt is to Francesca Wade's fantastic history *Square Haunting*, which introduced me to the women of Mecklenburgh Square in Bloomsbury, where Dorothy L Sayers and Virginia Woolf once lived. So too did Eileen Power, the first woman professor of economic history at the London School of Economics. I couldn't resist borrowing Eileen for my novel.

Other 'borrowings' include the model for the Caravanserai, which is based on the Caravan Club in Endell Street, London, which opened during the 1930s and was described by its respectable neighbours as 'an absolute sink of iniquity'!

I have tried to make the book true to the period, with research using the British Newspaper Archive, the British Library, The National Archives, The National Library of Scotland's wonderful online historical ordnance survey maps, the V&A Museum's costume collection, the Bow Street Police Museum and many more. Thanks to all who have helped. Errors are my own.

There are too many books to mention, but Nick Rennison's *1922: Scenes From A Turbulent Year* and the classic Robert

Graves/Alan Hodge *The Long Week-End: A Social History of Great Britain 1918 - 1939* were most useful.

If you're interested in the history behind *Blackmail In Bloomsbury*, look out my Stories Behind The Story blog on Substack, where I spill the beans on my research.

About the Author

Anna Sayburn Lane is a novelist and journalist who writes historical cozy mysteries and contemporary thrillers.

Anna studied English and History at university, then began her career as a reporter on a south London newspaper, later moving into medical journalism.

She published her first novel, the literary thriller *Unlawful Things*, in 2018, followed by *The Peacock Room* in 2020, *The Crimson Thread* in 2021 and *Folly Ditch* in 2022. *Unlawful Things* was shortlisted for the Virago New Crime Writer award and picked as a Crime in the Spotlight choice by the Bloody Scotland crime writing festival.

She recently switched to writing historical murder mysteries set in 1920s London. *Blackmail In Bloomsbury* is the first in the series, featuring apprentice detective Marjorie Swallow. It is followed by *The Soho Jazz Murders*, *Death At Chelsea* and *The Riviera Mystery.* More to come!

Anna lives on the Kent coast.

You can connect with me on:

🌐 https://annasayburnlane.com

🅕 https://www.facebook.com/annasayburnlane

Also by Anna Sayburn Lane

Step back into the roaring twenties with classic detective novels set in 1920s London. *Blackmail In Bloomsbury* is the first in the series featuring plucky apprentice detective Marjorie Swallow.

The Soho Jazz Murders

It's January 1923 and London feels dreary after the excitement of Christmas. So Marjorie is excited about meeting the American Ambassador's niece, a genuine 1920s flapper with a love of jazz, dancing and fun.

But their night out at Soho's infamous Harlequin Club comes to a tragic end. Soon Marjorie is working undercover as a dance hostess in the club to unmask the drugs gangs that threaten the West End. It's a perilous occupation - and there are more deaths to come.

The Soho Jazz Murders is the second in the 1920s murder mystery series, featuring the irresistible apprentice detective Marjorie Swallow.

Death At Chelsea

Detective duo Mrs Jameson and Marjorie Swallow are called to investigate when a famous gardener suspects that someone is sabotaging her priceless lilies, ahead of the 1923 Chelsea Flower Show.

But soon it's not just the flowers that are dying. Rival gardeners, intrepid plant hunters and King George V himself are caught up in a poisonous bouquet with its roots deep in the mountains of Tibet.

The third in the Marjorie Swallow 1920s Murder Mystery series takes readers to grand country houses, dodgy pubs serving Covent Garden flower market and – of course – all the glamour of Chelsea.

The Riviera Mystery

A September trip to the French Riviera sounds just the ticket for apprentice sleuth Marjorie Swallow. But when she steps aboard the famous Blue Train to the Mediterranean coast, she discovers this won't be an ordinary vacation.

Surrounded by diamond merchants, film stars and artists, Marjorie is swept off her feet by the beauty of the Côte d'Azur – and by one artist in particular. However, romance goes on hold when she's caught up in the aftermath of a death at a glamorous party.

Soon she's asking herself exactly who she can trust, as her investigations lead her down a twisting road of money, passion, art and murder.

Printed in Great Britain
by Amazon

51762748R00148